PRAISE FOR
THE LAST THING TO BURN

"Immediate, intense, gripping, taut, terrifying, moving, and brilliant."
—Lisa Jewell, #1 *New York Times* bestselling author of
The Night She Disappeared

"Brilliantly written . . . terrifying."
—Ruth Ware, #1 *New York Times* bestselling author of *One by One*

"I could not stop reading this! Brilliantly done . . . I'm awestruck!"
—Denise Mina, internationally bestselling author of *The Less Dead*

"This outstanding thriller by Will Dean might be the best book you read
this year. The Last Thing to Burn is intense, dark, and utterly chilling—I
felt this one in my bones."
—Jennifer Hillier, award-winning author of *Jar of Hearts* and
Little Secrets

"I couldn't put it down. A visceral nightmare of a book with one of the
most evil villains I've come across in a long time. Powerful writing."
—Steve Cavanagh, award-winning author of *The Defense*

"Ratchets up the tension to the point where I had to check my pulse."
—Liz Nugent, critically acclaimed author of *Little Cruelties*

"A heart-racing exploration about human survival. An addictive and in-
sightful thriller."
—Maxine Mei-Fung Chung, critically acclaimed author of
The Eighth Girl

"Brilliant."
—Elly Griffiths, internationally bestselling author of *The Night Hawks*

EMILY
BESTLER
BOOKS

ATRIA

An Imprint of Simon & Schuster, Inc.
1230 Avenue of the Americas
New York, NY 10020

First Emily Bestler Books/Atria Paperback edition January 2022

EMILY BESTLER BOOKS / ATRIA PAPERBACK and colophon are trademarks of Simon & Schuster, Inc.

For information about special discounts for bulk purchases, please contact Simon & Schuster Special Sales at 1-866-506-1949 or business@simonandschuster.com.

The Simon & Schuster Speakers Bureau can bring authors to your live event. For more information or to book an event, contact the Simon & Schuster Speakers Bureau at 1-866-248-3049 or visit our website at www.simonspeakers.com.

Interior design by Dana Sloan

Manufactured in the United States of America

5 7 9 10 8 6

Library of Congress Cataloging-in-Publication Data has been applied for.

ISBN 978-1-9821-5646-6
ISBN 978-1-9821-5647-3 (pbk)
ISBN 978-1-9821-5648-0 (ebook)

THE
LAST THING
TO BURN

A Novel

WILL DEAN

EMILY BESTLER BOOKS

—

ATRIA

New York • London • Toronto • Sydney • New Delhi

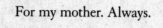

For my mother. Always.

"I should have chosen the moment before the arrival of my children, for since then I've lost the option of dying. The sharp smell of their sun-baked hair, the smell of sweat on their backs when they wake from a nightmare, the dusty smell of their hands when they leave a classroom, meant that I had to live, to be dazzled by the shadow of their eyelashes, moved by a snowflake, bowled over by a tear on their cheek."

—Kim Thúy, *Ru*

I'm not going back.

Not now, not ever. My right ankle is the size of a fist and I can feel bone shards scraping together, six-year-old shards, as I limp away from the farm cottage toward the distant road.

The destination is there, I can see it, but it's not getting any closer. I walk and hobble and it's still a whole world of pain away from where I am right now. My eyes scan the distant road, left, then right, for him. Very little traffic. Trucks transporting cabbages and sugar beets; cars ferrying fruit pickers. One bus a day.

I have my fiver, his fiver, my ticket out of this flatland hell. The creased green paper's rolled and tucked into my hair, still black after these nine long years though only God knows how.

Every step is a mile. Etched aches and new pains melt into red-hot misery beneath my right knee: boiling fat and razor-sharp icicles all at once.

The track is pale October brown, the mud churned and dried and churned by the tractor. His tractor.

I move as fast as I can, my teeth biting down onto my tongue. I'm balancing different pains. Managing best I can.

He's not coming. I can spot his Land Rover from a mile away.

I stop to breathe. The clouds are moving over me, urging me out of this forgotten place, helping me at my back, pushing me along toward that road, toward that one bus per day with his banknote hidden in my hair.

Is that?

No.

Please, no. It can't be.

I stand completely still, my anklebone throbbing stronger than my own heart, and he is there on the horizon. Is that his truck? Maybe it's just the same model. Some plow salesman or schoolteacher. I look right, toward the town past the bridge, and left, toward the village. Places I've never been to. My eyes lock onto the Land Rover. His Land Rover. Keep driving, for the love of God be someone else and keep on driving.

But he slows and then my shoulders fall.

He turns onto this track, his track, the track to his farm, to his land.

I look right at the nothingness, the endless fields he's sculpted, and the spires in the distance, and then left to the wind turbines and the nothingness there, and then back. That's when I weep. Tearless, noiseless weeping. I fall. I fold forward with a crack, a sharp stone beneath my right knee, a blessed distraction from my ankle.

He drives to me and I just kneel.

With a clean, clear-thinking head maybe I'd have managed to escape? Not with this leg. Not with him always coming back. Always checking on me. Always watching.

It's Kim-Ly in my head now and I will not let him in. My sister, my little sister, it is you who gives me the strength to breathe right now on this long, straight-churned mud track in this unseen flatland. I'm here for you. Existing so that you can carry on. I know what's to come. The fresh horrors. And I will endure them for you and you alone.

He stands over me.

Once again, I exist only in his shadow.

Consumed by it.

I won't look at him, not today. I think of you, Kim-Ly, with Mother's eyes and Father's lips and your own nose. I will not look up at him.

I've made it past the locked halfway gate.

But no farther.

It's still his land all around. Smothering me.

He bends and reaches out and gently picks me up off the dirt and he lifts me higher to his shoulder and carries me on toward the cottage.

I am as limp as death.

My tears fall to the mud, to the footprints I created an hour ago, the man's size eleven sandal prints; one straight, the other a right angle—that one a pathetic scrape more than a print, each step a victory and an escape and a complete failure.

He walks without speaking, his strong shoulder pressing into my waist, hard and plateaued. He holds me with no force. His power is absolute. He needs no violence at this moment because he controls everything the eye can see. I can feel his forearm at the back of my knees and he's holding it there as gently as a concert violinist might hold a bow.

My ankle is ruined. The nerves and bones and tendons and muscles are as one damaged bundle; sharp flints and old meat. Fire. I feel nothing else. The pain is something I live with every day of my life, but not like this. This is wretched. My mouth is open. A silent cry. A hopeless and unending scream.

He stops and opens the door that I scrub for him each morning and we go inside his cottage. I have failed and what will he do to me this time?

He turns and walks past the mirror and past the key box bolted high on the wall and heads into our one proper downstairs room. In Vietnam my family had six downstairs rooms. He takes me past the locked TV door and past the camera and places me down on the plastic-wrapped sofa like I'm a sleeping toddler extracted from some long car journey.

He looks down at me.

"You'll want a pain pill, I expect."

I close my eyes tight and nod.

"It'll come."

He takes the Land Rover keys from his pocket and walks to the key box in the entrance hall. He takes the key from the chain around his neck and opens the box and locks away the keys and then locks the box.

He comes back in. A man twice the size of my father but half the worth of a rat.

"Empty 'em."

"What?" I say.

"Empty your pockets, then."

I unzip his fleece, the zipper buckling as I sit hunched on his sofa, and reach down into my apron, his mother's apron, and pull out my remaining four objects, the four things I have left in the world that are actually mine.

"Four left."

I nod.

"Well, your fault, ain't nobody to blame but yourself, Jane."

My name isn't Jane.

"Pick one."

I look down at the plastic dust sheet covering the sofa, at the ID card, which contains the last words I possess in my own language, the last photo of myself, of what I used to look like before all this happened. It's the last thing with my real name, Thanh Dao; with my date of birth, November 3; with my place of birth, Biên Hòa, Vietnam. It proves I am really me.

Next to it lie Mom and Dad. My mother with her smiling eyes and her cowlick bangs and that half grin I see in my sister sometimes. And my father, his hand in hers, with love and trust and friendship and warmth shining onto my mother from his every pore, his every aspect.

And then Kim-Ly's letters. Oh, sweet sister. My life is your life now; my future belongs to you, use every second of it, every gram of pleasure. I stare down at the wrinkled papers and think of her Manchester days, her job, her hard-won independence, soon to be real, complete, irrevocable.

I inherited the fourth item from his mother. I didn't want it but I needed it. I need it still. I found it in the storage closet up in the small back bedroom, the one he makes me sleep in one week out of every four. *Of Mice and Men* is his mother's book but I've read from it or thought of it or wished from it every day for years so now, by rights, I'd say it belongs to me.

I look at him, at his lifeless blue-gray eyes.

"I need them Lenn, please." I mesh my fingers together. "Please, Lenn."

He paces over to the Rayburn stove and opens the fire door and pushes in a handful of coppiced willow and closes the door again and turns to me.

"You went leavin' here so now you choose one of 'em. If you don't, I will."

He goes over to the sink, and I see the jar on top of the cabinet.

"Can I have a pill first, please."

"Pick one and then you can take the pill."

My ID card. My photo of my parents. My sister's precious letters. My book. My, my, my, mine. Not his. Mine.

I already know which one it'll be. I've rehearsed this in my mind. In the middle of the night. Planning. Scheming. Hoping for the best while preparing for the worst. For this.

"You didn't even make it one-third out," he says. "Don't know what you were thinking, woman."

I focus on Mom's face. I memorize it through my ankle pain, through the hurt and the dry tears. I register the details. The asymmetry of her eyebrows. The warmth in her gaze. I look at Dad and scan his face and take in every mole and line, every beautiful wrinkle, every hair on his gentle head.

I push the photo toward Lenn and gather the letters and the book and the ID card back into my arms and onto my lap and bury them deep inside his mother's apron.

This was a selfish act. But I think my parents would understand. They'd know I needed the book to keep sane and the ID card to stay me and the letters to get up each morning and go to sleep each night. They'd forgive me.

He picks up the photo and holds it by the corners so as not to touch the image. He puts it inside his oil-stained overalls and then he stretches up and takes the jar off the kitchen cabinet. It looks like something you'd find in a candy store, tall and made from glass with a screw-on metal lid. It contains tablets the size of pencil erasers. He won't tell me exactly what they are but I know. He's a farmer. He can order them without anyone asking any questions. He takes out a pill, the white dust marking the cracks of his calloused fingertips like some rock climber or weight lifter, and then he snaps it in two. He places half back inside the jar and screws on the lid so tight I can't budge it, and then places the jar back on top of the cabinet. I've drugged him before, of course. Well, I tried to, did you think I wouldn't? Fragments dissolved into hot gravy. Almost two pills. But he's very particular about his food. He tasted something was off. By then he'd eaten most of his dinner. I watched him, praying, pleading, begging. He got sleepy, and then, dozy like a furious wasp at the end of summer, he came at me. That's how I lost my own clothes and the silver ring my grandmother gave me when I left home. He tasted the horse drugs in his chicken pie gravy. He's more careful these days.

"Have this."

He pours me a glass of water from the sink and hands it to me along with the snapped half pill and I take it and swallow it.

"Can I have the other half, please, Leonard?"

"You'll get poorly, you know you will."

The pill's taking effect slowly. I urge its haziness down my body toward my ankle, faster, willing it down there through the blood vessels and nerve pathways to dull the pain away.

"We'll see about the rest of that pill. Maybe after you've had dinner."

That is hope right there. The chance that I might black out, be swept away by the tide into a deep and dreamless sleep. He'll be watching me, monitoring me, he always is—gazing, staring, owning—but I will be at the bottom of the sea by then, a break from this fenland life, a sabbatical from hell.

"Better get the sausages on while I watch them tapes. I want 'em like me mother did 'em, proper brown and no pale bits."

I try to stand from the sofa but my ankle's too raw, even with the horse pill kicking in. I drag myself over to the fridge while he sits at the old PC, careful to unlock it with his password, his broad back shielding it from me. The screen lights up. Everything in his fridge is his food. Oh, I'll eat some of it, but I didn't buy or grow or pick or choose anything. I drop the sausages, Lincolnshire, into a cast-iron skillet on the Rayburn. He's scanning through the tapes, the tapes from the seven cameras installed by him in this house, his house, to monitor me every single day. The sausages spit in the pan. I watch the fat liquefy and boil inside the sausage skins, bubbles moving, and then one bursts open from its side and fizzes.

"You've had quite a day, ain't you?" he says, pointing to the screen, to me a few hours ago collecting my belongings, my four objects that are now three, and leaving this place through the front door.

"Quite the little holiday, you've had, eh?" He looks over at the potatoes in the sink. "Make sure there's no lumps in it this time, Jane." He turns back to the desktop screen. "Me mother's never had lumps. I don't like eatin' no lumps."

I put his plate down in front of him and place a fork by his glass of lime juice. He demands it the color of morning piss, his words, so that's what I give him.

"Looks alright," he says, eyeing up the plate. "We'll see."

I take my food and place it opposite him. I look down at it, at the browns and the beiges. I can't put too much pressure on my ankle so I cross my legs carefully and let my bad foot hang in midair like some botched medieval experiment.

"It's alright," he says, his mouth open, the food right there for me to see. "It'll do."

The half pill is kicking in now, it's draining my body of all feeling, lightening my head and fading all sharpness. I'm numbing.

He cuts his sausage with a fork, half crushing it, the coarse texture fanning under the prongs of his cutlery, and then he scoops up some of the mashed potatoes, lump free, as demanded, and pushes it into his mouth. The camera's on in the corner and the keys are locked away in the box.

"Mighty White," he says, not looking up at me.

I uncross my legs carefully and hobble to the bread bin, my good foot taking most of my weight. I place two slices onto a breadboard.

"Don't waste a plate for it, no point."

I limp over to the table and offer him the bread. He takes it and folds it and mops up the remaining mashed potatoes and eats it and swallows. He drains his lime juice.

"When me mother and me used to go to Skegness as a young'un, she'd cook us some sausages like them and it would be good, you know. Yours are gettin' better, not the same yet, but gettin' better. Bit more brownin' next time, maybe."

I nod and clear the plates.

"You done leaking yet or another day you reckon?"

I stop still, plates in hand, by the sink. I want to smash them all and use the shards to slice his neck. I've dreamed of it. Asleep and awake. The blood from his jugular vein hitting the plastic-covered sofa. The life leaving his massive body. The relief.

"Another day," I lie. He might check. He's checked before. Go ahead. Check.

"Right, no need for a bath then, just do the dishes and then we'll settle in for the night."

I scrape the plates, a piece of sausage skin stuck between my front teeth, and pile them on top of the old cast-iron skillet, his mother's skillet, and wash up. He won't buy me gloves because his mother never used gloves and that's why my hands look like this.

"I'm goin' up to feed the pigs, what we got?"

His damn pigs live better than I do. I look out the kitchen window, the small one above the sink, and I can see the pig barn in the far distance. Cinder-block walls and a corrugated roof. Far enough away that I can eclipse it with the tip of my thumb.

Off toward the sea, past the dike, there's nothing else except his pigs and the marshes. I take some scraps from the bin, some potato peelings, sausage gristle I couldn't chew through, some out-of-date presliced Spar shop ham from the fridge. I load it all into the scraps bucket and hand it over to him.

"Make up the fire for when I get back in, it's raw out and the clouds are lookin' nasty."

I wash up and listen for the front door.

That's it.

The noise of the bolt.

Blessed relief. I breathe out and wait, scouring pad in hand, and then he's there at the back field on his quad, a monster riding away on four wheels, riding off toward the pigs, his brethren. I wish upon him a heart attack and a bad fall, perhaps into the dike, drowning, the quad on top, and a lightning strike. But nothing ever happens to him, no consequence. He's as solid and as basic as a concrete wall. The times I've begged to all the gods, to the horizon, to the four spires I can see to the north on a clear day and the three to the south, to the wind turbines, for some retribution to be brought, some penalty, and yet he thrives on.

The tapes are rolling. They're always rolling. If I move they start recording, that's how he installed them. Leonard's quite handy with electrics and plumbing. And he may come back. He says he's off to feed the pigs, those royal animals luxuriating on their throne of filth, unaware of their relative freedom, but he could just as well race back in five minutes. To surprise me. To check up on me. To control his small world and keep things exactly as he likes them.

My three things are still in my apron, his mother's apron. With my back to the camera, I remove *Of Mice and Men* and prop it on the windowsill and read as I pretend to wash up. Comforting words. Hope. My eyes flick over the pages. I know all the text already. I glance up to the window and back, always checking. I think about George and Lennie's alfalfa patch, their rabbits, their dream, their escape, and I think of my sister, Kim-Ly. All of my potential futures are now invested in her one actual future. I will escape this place through her spirit and live on through her.

We arrived here together.

Nine years ago, and back then it was the rosiest thing that we could ever have imagined. It was sold to us well, the idea that we would travel to the United Kingdom to work good jobs—ten times Vietnamese wages—and send money back to our family. The two of us could work and it would be hard but we'd always have each other, wouldn't we? The two men who came to our house were profession-als. They had business cards and one had a leather briefcase. The boss smiled at my mother and shook my father's hand. They drank our tea. Those men sat and cast their spell and fed us their despicable lies. They sold us an impossible dream and they sold it very well, that alfalfa rabbit patch, that chance to look after the parents whose im-ages will be burned on the Rayburn stove in this place later tonight.

His Rayburn stove.

If it's in this house or on this land and it's not his, then it's hers, his mother's, and that's almost worse because she gave birth to him, she reared him, she created him.

I put the book back into my threadbare apron, the gray light from the window dwindling, the autumn mists rolling in off the salt marshes that are beyond my vision but that he tells me are out there after the pig barn and the copsewood. I smell the salt on the air some nights. I taste it. Something from far away. From beyond his influence. I turn my back on his pigs and on him and look at this pitiful downstairs room. Rayburn to my left, our oven and our cooktop, our light and our comfort, the heart of this rotten home. And then the small pine table with two pine chairs and the armchair next to the Rayburn, the shape of him preserved in the cushion for all eternity. And then the locked TV cabinet, and then the sofa with the plastic dust sheet. Aside from the entrance hall and the stairs up and the lean-to bathroom out the back, that's it, that's all there is down here.

I drag myself through the door and step down into the bathroom. It's damp back here, always. And cold, the floor has a chill alien to the land outside; it's frost-cold for six months of the year and wet to the touch. He built the room himself in his forties, eight years ago, after his first wife died. I don't close the door because that's a rule.

At least tomorrow I get a hot bath. Scalding hot, water heated from the back boiler behind the Rayburn stove, red hot, kettle hot. I take it just as close to boiling as I can stand. Burn me, numb my brain stem, help me take away these feelings. The downside is what will happen afterward.

The cold of this room, the damp of it. My sister and I arrived in Liverpool inside a shipping container nine years ago. It was the coldest time of my life. From the heat of Saigon to that icy metal box. Seventeen of us hiding behind packages and crates. Me clinging to my sister and to the backpack I had with me. The photos of my parents. Sixteen of us made it to Liverpool, and I sometimes wish, I often wish, that I had been the seventeenth.

I pull myself upstairs, heaving my weight with my arms, clinging to the banister like I'm fighting in a tug-of-war, creeping up one bare step at a time. I need the second half of that pill, my ankle's screaming out for it. I've only passed out once in my life from pain and that was the day this happened to my ankle.

There are two bedrooms in this place, his place. His room, which he calls our room, faces the front, toward the track I failed to walk out from today, and the locked halfway gate and the silos and barns and yards and old plows. There's a storage heater and a wardrobe and a double bed. The other, smaller bedroom, the back bedroom, is my room one week out of every four.

For those six days, more or less, I get to sleep on my own. He will not tolerate me in his front bedroom. These are the days I live for, the nights I get to sleep in my own space and dream my own dreams. These are the days when I can almost exist.

But I have to keep the back bedroom door open at all times. That's another rule.

Always open. And he's pushed the single bed up against the wall so he can watch me from the landing or from his front bedroom. He wanders in whenever he feels like it. I have no security of space, no boundaries of my own whatsoever. Nothing to protect or hide behind. I have no privacy, not even anything resembling it. I am filmed and observed and caught out and recorded and spied upon. I live in an open prison surrounded by wall-less fields and fenceless fens. It's the vastness of these flatlands that keeps me prisoner here. I'm contained, incarcerated in the most open landscape of them all.

I can hear his quad. I rush into the storage closet in the small back bedroom. The left side's for me. It was full when I arrived here from the other farm. Seventeen possessions. Now down to just three. The opposite shelves, on the right side, store his mother's old things. He's never bought me anything. I have to make do with his mother's woolens and her underwear and her blankets. I can't wear her shoes, I can't really wear any shoes at all, so I wear his open sandals, his old ones, with one leather part snipped open to allow for my disfigured knot of a foot.

I put my ID card and my book and my sister's letters down on the slatted shelves. This side of the closet looks sad. Almost empty now. An egg timer running out of sand. Then I pick up the letters, seventy-two of them, and hold them to my upper lip, to the soft skin beneath my nose, and I breathe her in.

"Where are you?" he shouts from the front door.

"Coming."

I arrive in the living room as he's pulling off his boots in the entrance hall and unlocking the key box with his neck key. He deposits the quad key in the box and yes, of course, I've tried to hot-wire it. I had no idea what I was doing, four years ago, maybe five, failed totally and that's when I lost my pencil, already shaved to a nub; that's when he took it and burned it in front of my eyes. I haven't written a word since.

"Get the kettle on, it's blowin' a gale out there."

I put the kettle on the Rayburn hot plate.

"Right, let's get this done, then." He pulls the photo of my parents out from his overalls. The tips of his fingers are red and his cuticles are bleeding. "Get the stove open."

I pull the door open to reveal glowing embers.

He holds up the photograph but it's gone to me already; I've made my peace. He licks his lips. "Don't do it again, Jane."

My name is not Jane.

"Do it again and you'll have nothin' left to burn in that stove, will you?"

I look at the embers.

He places the photo in, but before he even releases it the edges curl and distort from the heat and then there's a contained white flash, an uneventful flaring from the burning willow, and then they're gone, transformed into heat to warm his bleeding hands and to make his beige sweet tea. They are gone.

I feel nothing.

I pour hot water into two mugs as he unlocks the TV cabinet in the corner of the room. I say cabinet, but it's a full-size door bolted to the walls in the corner on a diagonal. It creaks as he opens it.

He locks the TV key in the key box and sits down in his armchair with his remote control to watch his TV.

He says "thanks," as I place his pesticide company freebie mug down by his chair.

"*Match of the Day*," he says. "One of your favorites, ain't it?"

I look back at the pills, the horse pills, cow pills, whatever they are, on the cabinet. Tranquilizers not tested on or for human beings. Generic medication for swine and bovines.

"Can I have the other half, please, Lenn?"

He takes a quick look at my right ankle, at the teeming mass of sinew and bone, at the pain contained within, at the bruising, the blood pooling at the base of my foot under the wretched skin, at the foot existing at ninety degrees, my foot, my sideways foot.

"Get the stove door open and heat this room, it's freezin' in here."

He stands up and reaches for the glass jar and unscrews the cap, the muscles in his hairless forearm flexing and bulging, and then he passes me the other half of the horse pill. I take it and open the door to the Rayburn so, in some feeble, distorted way, the room, this one room, his room, is transformed, in his eyes at least, and only his, into a cozy living room.

"What do you say?"

"Thank you, Lenn."

He sits back down in his armchair and I sit the way he likes me to sit, on the floor by his knees. By his feet. He watches *Match of the Day* with subtitles on, some early gift from him to me so I could improve my English, and he pats my hair.

"It's alright, ain't it, this life?" He sips his beige tea and the fire from the stove lights one side of his face. "We're warm, under a decent roof, full bellies, together, not all bad, is it?"

I sit, my crushed ankle throbbing, his broad, rough fingers in my hair, patting my head, and I swallow the half pill.

3

I wake up, but not like you would.

There's a sense that I'm not asleep anymore, but I have distance from that sense, I am away from it.

And then the pain hits.

It doesn't creep up on me like you might expect it to. From deep, sedated horse-pill sleep, not sleep really, more like an amateur coma, to screaming pain. I look down. I'm in the back bedroom of his cottage under his mother's bedsheet and my ankle's almost twice the size it usually is. My toes are black with blood. I'm lying flat on my back and my left foot is sticking up like yours would and my right foot is lying away from me, attached, somehow, some fused knot of broken bones, glued splinters, into a ball of an ankle, an abomination of a joint.

I need another half pill.

More numbness. More distance and more fog.

The clock on the wall says it's half past eleven and I can hear his tractor through the loose timber window frames and I can feel the draft off his fields.

I drink a sip of water and try to stand. My ankle has the color and ripeness of some long-forgotten soft fruit. It feels less cohesive than usual today after my walk, my failed not even halfway walk. It feels like it might crumble and fall apart if I put any weight on it.

I hop but that's worse. My right foot dangles and bobs and the strain is too much and I sit back down on the end of the bed, sweat beading on my forehead and at the back of my neck; my face twisted.

The tractor's close by, maybe the ten-acre field to the east, maybe the winter wheat field edged by the long dike.

I straighten myself and pull my body down the stairs one step at a time, one agony at a time. The fragments inside my ankle joint scrape, and when I reach the bottom I hear a dull crack.

The day is vague.

Overcast.

I'm standing by the front door, the damp breeze cooling my pain, my eyes on his tractor plowing his fields, the outline of his head visible in the tractor cab, and I can still make out my one-day-old footprints in the dirt, each one a victory and a defeat.

He stops the tractor and climbs down.

Growing ever larger as he walks toward me.

"You woke up, then?"

"I need a pill," I say, my teeth gritted.

He walks closer and then past me into the kitchen. He gives me half a pill and I take it.

"You gonna get behind, better get crackin'."

"I will."

He makes coffee: one for me and one for him. He reuses his pesticide company mug and gives me a floral thing his mother used to like. Nescafé and two sugar lumps. The flowers on the porcelain are faded to the point of near extinction. My hands have scrubbed these mugs and Jane, his mother, scrubbed them, and Jane, his first wife, she scrubbed them as well.

The pill kicks in. I'll push him to change to three-quarters soon. He can snap off the end and give me the big portion of the pill. He can do that three days running. On the fourth day he can give me the three snapped-off end pieces. It'll be convenient for him and better for me. I can manage it then. I'll carry on for Kim-Ly.

I push coppiced willow into the Rayburn stove and stoke it. The water on the top begins to simmer.

The bathroom floor is as cold as a puddle in February. It's soft, that's the thing, not just the damp or the chill, but it's spongy like he laid the linoleum straight onto mud. And the smell. Some sort of decay. Rot. The ground under this bathroom is poor ground and the smell is so pungent it makes me retch.

I comb my hair, and then he's there at my back watching me. He's standing at the base of the stairs, but there's a rule that I must keep all internal doors open. And he's watching me comb my hair, watching my back. Tonight he'll tell me to run a bath. This is why I tried to leave yesterday, the last day of my period, the last chance before it happened all over again. I was going to use my banknote, the one I lodged in the storage heater in the small back bedroom, to call someone. Anyone. I took the money almost a year ago. I don't know who to call. Someone in Manchester? Someone to find her and tell her to hide. To flee. Because if I had escaped, then he'd have called his friend Frank Trussock. They'd have had her sent straight back, and then all her toiling, all her work and sacrifice to pay back the men who shipped us here, who tricked us—it'd all be for nothing.

Lenn leaves and closes the front door and drives away.

I make toast on the Rayburn with his Mighty White bread. The package doesn't say Mighty White but that's what he calls it so that's what I call it. Mighty White. It's like eating wall insulation but I'm used to it now. I'm accustomed to it. I've grown to enjoy it, even.

The pain's dull and so is my head. This is why my memories are split like a ruined sauce. I can find blobs of this, recall strands of that, but it's an unruly mess. How I got here, who I am, what he's done to me. I remember his rules. That's not an issue. I remember his rules and his meal schedule, what he eats each day of the week, and how he likes his ham, eggs, and fries. It's myself that I forget sometimes. Who I really am. From before. But I still have my book and my ID card and my letters.

I load the old washing machine with cloths. They're his mother's too. I begged him in the early days to buy tampons or sanitary napkins when he went to the Spar shop in the village each week to buy food. He said, "Me mother never needed no fancy rags and you don't neither." It's an insult, a degradation so personal that it made me ill. I have to use his mother's towels, the moth-eaten cloths she used for herself and then used as diapers for him. They've been on both of them and now I have to wear them. I'm used to it now. It's the price I pay for five or six quiet nights in the small back bedroom each month alone with my own thoughts and my own beautiful memories.

The main room camera's on me as I remove the cloths from the washing machine and take them outside. My apron, his mother's apron, flaps in the damp fenland breeze as I walk to the line joining his house to his shed. I hang up the cloths with his mother's wooden clothespins, and as I secure each one to the plastic line I study the horizon. If you've ever seen a photo taken from the edge of space, then you'll know what I'm looking at. That gentle curvature. Imagined or real. That sense of the edge of the world. There are four spires in this direction and two are obscured by his toolshed from here. Spires, churches, ancient trees, my salvation, places I've run toward before my leg, before all this, in the early days. I never made it past his fields. All his. From here they are endless, one after the other, each one vast and featureless, the hedges tall enough to block out almost everything beyond.

A blackbird beats its wings and flies away toward the sea.

I hobble back to the house and see a glint of bright green in the crack between the stones. He's far enough away, I think. There's time. I get to the wall and chisel out the hard candy I deposited a few months back. I say deposited because this is my bank account, my savings, my safety-deposit box of stored happiness, the only tiny joys that I am really in control of, that I can meter out and ration and use up as I see fit.

He gives them to me from time to time. A carrot as opposed to a stick. He gives me one from the window of his Land Rover like I'm a beggar or a small child. Sometimes I eat it immediately if I can't see past the end of that day. Sometimes I secrete it into a wall or into the nook of a tree. They get damaged, sure they do. The ones on the south side of the house melt in the summer sun so that they become as misshapen as my right foot. The edges change and fill the gaps like the smallest stained-glass windows ever imagined. The ones in the trees sometimes get nibbled at by squirrels and insects. But on the days when I have nothing, the days when the skies are pitiless and dour, then at least I have my hard candies and I draw down from those deposits and I savor them.

I put the green candy on my tongue. A miniature rebellion.

I hobble around the outside of the cottage, small as it is, my arm skirting the dusty yellow stones, and take in the full terror of my existence. Sweet green in my mouth, some approximation of a remembered apple, and flatlands all around. With my back to the bathroom the view is almost empty. Toward the sea. I can't see the water from here, I can't smell the salt today, but I can sense it's there just like humans have been able to sense since the beginning of time. The land is flat but it also slopes at some undetectable angle. It gently slips away.

I stare out at his pig barn. Damn pigs. I seldom hear them but when I do they sound deranged. When the wind blows in off the sea and the air is right, then I can hear their desperate hungry squeals as he feeds them. Distant, very faint, but I can hear those pigs as he cares for them.

I skirt around the chimney warm from the Rayburn on the other side of the wall, and I see the ash pile: burned willow and burned possessions. Past it I see the wind turbines. I'm careful not to bite down on this green candy, it must melt slowly, its sugars pooling with my saliva, me prolonging this earned pleasure.

He's coming back.

I swallow the candy and go inside and start scrubbing the floors with hot water and soap.

"Now then," he says.

I look up from the floor, my right leg splayed behind me like it doesn't belong.

"Be back for me lunch in a bit."

That's the thing with farmers, or some farmers at least—they're always dropping in. For keys, for a coffee, to fetch a hat, to eat lunch. They're always on the farm, and if they're not then you never know when they'll return. I have no control over my doors or my food or my body or my clothes or my anything.

I watch him from the kitchen sink window as he drives off toward the pigs with his plow high in the air behind his decrepit old tractor. He tells me the *farm barely wipes its face,* by which he means it only just breaks even each year. No money to upgrade equipment so he has to fix and make do. Lunch today will be a cheese sandwich, presliced, on Mighty White, also presliced, with a brown pickle. He makes me take out all the bits so it's the consistency of thin gravy. I eat the bits. Then he'll have an apple and a glass of lime juice. I have offered to grow food, to save him money, but he refuses. *Sell it in the shop*, he says.

The camera watches me as I scrub down the bathroom, the toilet with its cracked cistern, and the cold iron bathtub. I bleach it but the stains remain. Brownish-red near the drain. The mold spores bloom every now and then and need to be scoured off the ceiling with Brillo pads and painted over with special sealant paint. The camera follows me.

It's starting to rain.

Fresh air and the cool scent of water on earth.

I get to the front door, need to bring the cloths in off the line, but there's someone there. On his track. In my day-old footprints. She's already past the locked halfway gate and I can see her car parked up by the barns and the old combine and she's walking toward me. He'll intercept her, of course. There's no way she'll make it all the way here. I've had a grain deliveryman almost reach this cottage twice, Jehovah's Witnesses once, and what looked like a school group almost made it to the front door, but he always intercepts, he's good at it. He almost always has perfect visibility on his land. I wait on the doorstep, my heart hard at the back of my chest. If she comes closer maybe I'll scuttle up the stairs and get my ID card and show it to her. Try to explain this horror. But I know I won't do it. I can't. Kim-Ly has almost paid off her debt and soon she'll be free to live a proper life in Manchester. She'll be free to make friends and have a family of her own. She'll control her things. Have the key to her own door and the option to do whatever she wants on her days off. She can watch the programs she enjoys, and maybe one day she'll come back and find me here in this open prison.

The woman smiles as she approaches. A broad, easy smile. Her red hair is dark from the rain. She's wearing a fleece and cream-colored jodhpurs, the kind horse riders wear. He'll intercept her soon, he'll swoop by on his quad and escort her away.

But he doesn't.

He's not here.

"Glad you're in," she says.

I nod and turn slightly so my bad foot is hidden behind the door.

"Sorry to bother you," she says, smiling and frowning. "I couldn't drive all the way up so I parked my Beetle in your yard up there, by the gate, I hope that's alright."

Help me.

"Damp day, isn't it?" She pauses. Focuses her eyes. "Is everything okay?"

Help me.

"It's just that, sorry"—she holds out her hand—"how rude, my name's Cynthia, Cynthia Townsend, nice to meet you."

I shake her hand.

"My name is Jane."

My name is not Jane. My name is Thanh Dao.

"Nice to meet you, Jane, lovely spot you've got here. I just moved into one of the old council houses in the next village, you know the ones, with the triangular windows above the doors?"

I nod.

I do not know the ones.

I have never been to the next village. The one with old council houses with triangular windows above the doors.

"Anyway, I just moved up here and I'm thinking of getting a horse, just for fun, you know, a tired old thing, nothing too frisky, just to walk around, and for company, really."

I nod.

"I just wondered if you might know anyone who'd rent me a paddock with water and a stable, nothing fancy, only I'd rather it wasn't too far from the village."

Help me.

The voice screams fiercely inside me. Deep inside. But on the surface I'm composed. Lenn once told me that if he ever caught me talking to a stranger he'd not let the stranger live. He'd bury them out in the marshes. So I have to stay calm. For this woman and for Kim-Ly. I must stay strong for them both.

"Or if you might have some land, just a small field. I'd be no bother."

He'll be back any second, taking her away and smiling and walking her to her car at the locked halfway gate and suggesting that maybe Frank Trussock's farm up near the bridge might have a paddock and they've got some decent stables up there, they used to have a livery stable back in the day.

But he doesn't come.

I start to sweat.

"Have a think about it if you would," she says.

I think I want her to take me away from this flatland hell, but then Kim-Ly will be sent back, disgraced, with the full debt to repay, with threats made to my family, threats that would be made real. We each had eighteen thousand to pay back to the men that brought us over. Kim-Ly's almost paid hers off, almost. Another two years and one month. She has to pay the apartment owner and the car driver and interest and other living fees, but she'll be away from it all soon. Free. Two more years.

I shake my head.

"No, you don't know anyone?" she says. "Or no, you don't have a paddock?"

I almost want him to come back now, to end this charade, this failed rescue, this lifeline dangled right in front of my face that I'm forced to ignore; this woman, this kind-faced red-haired woman called Cynthia who I need to tell nothing to for the sake of my baby sister, for her life.

"You'll have to ask my husband, Lenn." He's not my husband. He's nothing. "Lenn will know."

"Is he around? Can I speak with him today?"

I shake my head.

She peers past me into the one downstairs room with its Rayburn stove and table for two and locked TV cabinet and old desktop PC.

"Are you sure everything's okay?" she asks.

I am torn inside. I crave to tell her but I bite down on my tongue.

"Fine," I say. "Everything's fine. Come back when Lenn's around and he'll help you."

She smiles with her face and her eyes and her cheeks, all lines and freckles, and I think she's beautiful in a gentle, slightly messy way.

"Okay, then. Thanks, Jane, have a nice weekend, won't you? See you around the area, I expect."

And with that, she smiles again and turns and her red hair shines in the shallow fen light and she walks away, normal pace, nothing like me yesterday, no scrapes on the right-hand side of the track. And she's gone.

My heart's punching out at my rib cage from within.

The sensation of tears but none come.

I close the door.

But what more could I have done?

I want more pills to dull my life but then I'll never get out of this place and he'll do whatever he wants. Whenever he wants. It's a horrific balance. Numb enough to carry on but not too numb that I lose all control. I have to tell her, this Cynthia. I can't let this opportunity pass. I bite my lip and open the front door.

Cold air.

She's there. Her back. Her red hair.

I open my mouth.

I scream but it's just a whine, an empty, silent whine. My leg aches, my hip aches, my right side, all the bones completely misaligned, it all aches. But also my heart and my mind and my gut. My soul. I sense my shoulders droop as I close the door and look up at the camera on the wall. Lenn'll be happy with how I handled this, how I got her away from his farm so fast. My sister will be okay because I did the right thing. She'll be one fraction closer to living a normal life. Today I obeyed his rules and now she will be safe.

In the past five nights, all except for last night, because of the horse pill, the whole horse pill, I've reread her letters. My sister writes the most wonderful letters. They're always two sides of A4, folded into three. She asks me questions even though I never answer, it's against the rules, and I love her for that. She cares. It's the closest thing I get to a proper conversation. She asks me if I talk to our parents much and if I'd heard that our little brother won a prize at school. She asks me if I'm seeing anyone. If I'm in love. She tells me about the work she does at the nail salon, the repeat customers, the unkind women who ignore her completely, the kind women who remember her name, her English name, the name given to her by her boss. My sister's name is not Sue.

And I'll reread the letters in three weeks' time when I get to sleep in my own room again, not mine, his, but my space at least when he's not barging in to watch me undress for bed or watch me sleep or watch me brush my hair with his mother's brush.

Cynthia.

I think her name is perfect for her. She has Cynthia freckles and Cynthia horsey jodhpurs and Cynthia wellies and Cynthia lipstick and a Cynthia fleece. She could never be called anything else. The way her name rolls around on my tongue. The image I have of the word, and of her. To say her name suits her is an understatement. Her name fits like a key in a lock. I need to think about what to say if she does come back, what to do. I need to plan. Can I ask her to get a message to Kim-Ly somehow? Without him finding out? Without Cynthia trying to be a hero and ruining everything for my little sister?

"Plow's all mucked up," says Lenn as he opens the door, breaking the spell. "Muck gets everywhere, don't it?"

He hangs up his jacket and pulls off his boots. I can see tiny flecks of winter wheat seed speckling the mud stuck to the rubber treads. Each seed shines. The hard outer shell of each grain reflects what little dull light exists in this room and I see each one of them.

"Make me a sandwich. I know it's early but make it anyhow."

He'll see the tapes before dinner like he has every day for the last seven years. Should I tell him about Cynth now or let him wait?

I take his Mighty White from his mother's enamel bread bin. I untie the see-through bag and make his sandwiches. Six. Margarine and presliced mild cheddar cheese and presliced cooked ham. I hold the margarine knife in my hand and look at it and imagine his neck like I've imagined it a hundred times before. I place it down. He likes his sandwiches cut on the diagonal into little triangles that look like the kites we flew as children on the hills above our town. I set a bag of salted chips, never opened, on the plate. Lime juice the color of piss. I place it all down on the table.

"Bitter out there, ain't it? Never a good wind from the east, never a good'un."

"A woman came."

"What?"

I sit down opposite him.

"A woman came by to rent a field for a horse."

"For a what?"

He stares at me.

"Horse," I say.

"An 'orse?"

I nod.

"What did you tell her then? Every word. What did you say to this lass?"

"That she would need to speak to you about it."

He looks at my eyes one at a time, back and forth, and then he picks up his sandwich, tiny in his filthy hand, and takes a bite.

"She comes back"—he swallows his mouthful—"and I'm not around, you keep the door locked and get yourself up them stairs, you hear me?"

I nod.

"No more chattin' with nobody, you hear me?"

I nod.

"Keep the front door locked or I'll keep you upstairs till spring."

"Okay."

He eats the rest of his lunch as I wash up, and then I bleach the sink and clean the surfaces. He puts his boots back on and puts his jacket back on.

"I can see everywhere from anywhere on me farm, Jane," he says. "Every corner. It's as flat as a dinner plate and I'm always here. Don't forget it."

I spend three hours sewing and repairing his shirts and his socks and some of his mother's cloths now that they're dry. With every puncture of steel needle through fabric I imagine it's his skin. Rough. Punctured all over. Dying. I drink beige tea, I'm used to it now, and I think some more about Cynthia. Maybe she has a boyfriend. A man who listens to her, really listens. Someone to remember her birthday and hug her when she's tired. A man to lean on and who's man enough to lean on her. Maybe she has someone like that in her life. I know she has a car, a VW Beetle, and maybe she has a job she enjoys, something she finds interesting. My mother was a teacher in Vietnam and she adored it. She still passes men and women in the street and they say *Can you remember me?* and she says *Of course I can* and they say *You were my favorite teacher.* That's a beautiful everyday thing. It's a legacy.

He comes back in when it's dark and tells me I'll get a bath tonight. He reviews the tapes as I'm cooking his, our, cod in parsley sauce with boiled potatoes and frozen Birds Eye peas. The pans are on the Rayburn stove and the firebox is full of thin logs. He lingers over Cynthia, or rather, as he can't see her on the tape, the camera doesn't pick up anything from outside, he lingers on me talking to her. Back bent over. His massive hand covering the mouse in its entirety. He's replaying the tapes and watching me as I wait for his boil-in-the-bag fish to heat up. Why do people here boil their food in plastic bags?

We eat. He mushes his overcooked cod pieces into the sauce and the potatoes and peas so it's one big goop, and then he shovels it all into his mouth with his fork.

The phone rings.

We both look at it, or rather, the heavy metal box covering it that he's bolted to the floor joists. The wires go down through the floorboards into the half-cellar. The desktop PC is connected to the outside world through this telephone line. It rings and the box shakes and we both stare at it. Who'd ring this man?

The phone stops.

"Get that bath run while you wash these plates up."

I do as he says.

Instead of me sitting by his feet while he watches TV, I wash the plates and then I undress and then I climb into the steaming-hot bath. He's there watching my every move but I do not acknowledge him. He's invisible to me. Irrelevant. I have to be careful not to slip. I let my arms support me as I climb in and settle down, my eyes focused on the water and not on him. My deformed ankle slips under the surface and out of sight and the pain changes. It doesn't go away but it's underwater now.

He comes into the room as I'm scrubbing my skin. The soft floor compresses under his weight. He's holding a mug of tea and he's watching me, taking sips, his eyes darting to my face, then to my body, then back to my face. Then he leaves and I can hear the news program begin.

The bath is good. Piping hot. Clean. I let my mind wander to whatever Kim-Ly is doing right now in Manchester. In her last letter she told me the nail salon is open later these days, until eight on Fridays to take advantage of women, some men but mainly women, who want a manicure before heading out for a fun evening with friends. I like to think of her going out on a Friday as well. She tells me there's a Chinatown in Manchester and she can find some of the fruits and herbs of home, not the same, but similar. She can buy *quýt* and long *nhãn* and *bưởi*. She can buy *ngò* and *húng cây*. Maybe she can make something wonderful out of it all. A recipe from our mother's mother. Something to take her back home for a few moments.

But this hot bath also marks the beginning of a long night and the beginning of the next three weeks in his front bedroom.

I dry off and pull on my nightie, his mother's nightie, and keep a small towel wrapped around my hair. I pull myself upstairs and sit on the end of his bed.

The TV goes quiet.

Footsteps.

I dry my hair, rubbing at it with his mother's towel.

He's washing himself downstairs in the bathroom. I can hear the water draining away into the fields and into the dikes and into the sea. I open his mother's linen closet and take out a fresh cotton sheet, and this one is older than the rest, it's almost see-through like muslin cheesecloth. I throw it into the air to unfold it and let it settle gently on the bed.

He'll need his special towel. I lay it on the right-hand side of the bed. He's brushing his teeth down there. Spitting. Gargling. I hear the toilet flush and then the bottom stair creak.

"Good bath, was it?"

He says bath with as short an "a" as you could possibly imagine. Other people say "baaath" and some say "baath," I do, and he says "bath." If the letter "a" could be any narrower, any more compressed, then that's the letter "a" that he pronounces.

I nod and pull my nightie, his mother's nightie, up over my head.

He looks.

I stare straight ahead.

I lay on the bed and pull the thin cotton sheet over myself. I adjust it so the sheet's covering me from the navel and higher. This is, in some ways, the worst of it. The waiting. Because it drives the truth home like a hammer would drive a nail through a plank of rotten wood. I have no say in this. None. I fought the first dozen times. The first hundred. I fought and pleaded and struck him. I scratched at his thick hide and I bit him so hard one time he jumped in the air. He's not a violent man, not usually, but he'll always take what he wants in his own horrifically gentle way.

I wait under the sheet. The single light bulb over the bed is on, it's always on for nights like this, and I look through the cotton and see him looking back down at me. He undresses, folding his jeans and his socks and his shirt and placing them by the linen closet. Still watching.

My head turns to the right under the sheet. It's an automatic response now, a learned coping mechanism. My entire existence is a learned coping mechanism.

Does he plan this? Does he think about me? I never want to be inside his thoughts. I want pain to strike him if he ever thinks of me.

The skin on my legs is chill.

He steps closer to me and I can feel his thighs against my feet, and the bed creaks and the mattress moves slightly.

I am as still as a marble statue of myself and just as dead. Just as cold.

I close my eyes and initiate what I think of as a mental epidural. It's all I have.

I claim my body from the navel and higher. This is me. The rest is not me. From the navel and higher I can think what I want and be who I want to be. Anything covered by this sheet, his mother's sheet, is me.

It's now I try to go back home. To the weekend feasts my mother and father would prepare for us. My brother and my sister and I would sit around the food. Neighbors would drop in, my mother's colleagues might come, we'd have uncles and aunts invite themselves. The spread was unimaginable. A mosaic of colors and sauces and herbs. Every taste catered to. I try to recall the scents and the spices and the noodle broths and the fruit, but my taste buds have been worn down as if they're oak nubs and they've been sanded each night.

He climbs onto the bed.

I sink as his weight bears down into the mattress.

When I think of Kim-Ly now she's in Manchester, out with friends, maybe even on a date. They'll get *phở* if it's available and salad rolls, and they'll drink ice-cold beers straight from the bottle. They might see a film. They'll laugh and she'll be able to say whatever she wants. Do whatever she wants. She'll be wearing her own clothes and walking without pain and she'll be making plans for her future.

His face is close to my shoulder and I can smell his soap through the cotton sheet, but the epidural is holding. I will not let this happen to me. I can't do anything about the rest, but the navel up is mine and I am somewhere else right now. He'll pay the price for his deeds in this life or the next.

My sister and I thought we'd be working in a shop, that was the deal my parents negotiated. With an agent who'd check up on us once a month. What a joke. They said there'd be substantial travel costs to cover, we knew that, and living costs afterward, but we were guaranteed retail work and we were guaranteed we'd be able to stay together.

And then they took us in a van from the container to the first farm.

We worked for twelve hours a day six days a week. We had to live there in a wooden shed. But we had a shower and toilet block

and we had decent food and they paid us. Not much after the accommodation costs and the interest and the random extra charges,
but we received an envelope each Friday. We had a day off to rest.
And most important, we had each other. We wrote to our parents
and they wrote back to us. It was a start. And then the day came
when they took Kim-Ly away, and they sold me to Lenn.

He rolls off me to the side and then the bed begins to shake. He
can't finish with me. He can't do it. He has to roll off and finish
himself. He uses the towel. I count this as a minor victory, a hollow
one, the most Pyrrhic victory of them all.

And then it's over. I let the epidural wear off and reclaim my
lower half. I wriggle to the end of the bed, him still next to me in the
fetal position, and I pull on my nightie, and walk out and grip the
banister and hobble down to the bathroom.

I feel sick. Always. Sick to my very core.

I keep the bathroom door open because that's the rule. But he'll
stay up there for a while now, he always does. At least I have that. A
window of relative privacy. I clean myself. Perhaps it's time to move
up to three-quarters of a horse tablet, pig tablet, cow tablet, whatever they are. It's too much for me to be this aware every day. I need
more escape. More numbness. I'll ask him tomorrow.

The toilet seat is ice-cold and the floor, the linoleum floor, is soft
and lumpy. The door is open but he won't come down. This is a
relatively safe time. He'll stay up there rolled into a ball on the bed
with that small towel. I look down at my feet. My right ankle is
swollen and my toes are pointing to the bathtub instead of straight
ahead. The house is silent. No electric boiler here like we had back
home. No air-conditioning unit. The place is deathly quiet. Lost
and alone in the flatlands.

I almost re-smashed my ankle a few years ago, I don't remember when exactly. I'd had enough. My plan was to reset the bone,

to allow it to fuse with the foot in the correct forward position, to recuperate, and then to flee. I almost went through with it. Desperate and stupid as it would have been. I sat on the small back bedroom floor with his claw hammer by my side. I lifted it and placed it back down. Felt the weight of the head. The smooth, oiled wood of the handle. I was ready to hit my swollen ankle, to undo and redo some of the damage. I was ready to twist my torso and lift the heavy head and swing and smash it into my own body. But I couldn't go through with it.

Before my ankle injury life was god-awful but it was better than this.

Before my ankle injury I could walk and I could jump and I could pivot and I could simply step into a bathtub.

Before my ankle injury there was always hope. Always a chance I could run away.

He's probably asleep up there now so I won't rush. If I wait awhile I'll be able to sneak in and maybe I can sleep without him getting anywhere near me, with my head facing away from him, with my eyes to the wall, with his breath nowhere near mine.

I stare up at the mold spores on the bathroom ceiling.

My first escape attempt, all those years ago, was almost my last.

I took thirteen possessions, all I had left at that time. I still owned my own sneakers and normal clothes and I had my purse and my card with telephone numbers written down on it.

The preparations were thorough. I knew exactly what I'd say to the first person I met. How to ask for help. To take me to a police officer. I thought through how I'd struggle and fight if I met one of his friends. If I bumped into Frank Trussock from the farm up by the bridge. I was optimistic. It was my time to leave.

I was maybe four hundred yards from the road when he spotted me.

There were cars and trucks, not many but some, driving from left to right and from right to left on the horizon. I could hear their engines. The sounds as they changed gears. There was a sign to this very farm, his farm, on the side of the road. It's too far away and too small for me to see from here. There was a green bus approaching in the far distance and I was running, I used to be a good runner. I was sprinting. But he got to me.

I fought him, I was stronger back then. With my head bent toward the bus I yelled for help, but my voice was carried on the winds back out to his farm and out to sea. I wriggled and scratched and bent my body this way and that to evade him. I kicked like a mule and I screamed, but his rough hands smothered me and he loaded me into his Land Rover as if I was a child mid-tantrum. He took me back to the house and he was angry, although he didn't show it. He didn't say a word in the Land Rover. But he was bleeding from his neck and I could see his hands were tense on the steering wheel. I'd almost escaped. He took me into the toolshed next to the house and my leg twitches just thinking about it. He took me into the shed and sat me down on the tool bench and he took a pair of steel bolt cutters off the wall. There was no glee in his expression. No fury. He was calm, like this all made sense. I remember begging him. I didn't fight, he was too strong for me, and I was too exhausted, and we were too far away for any mortal soul to hear. I begged him for my life. He told me about his rules and about how much I'd cost him. He told me this was for my own good. That things would be better and simpler from then on. No more messing about. And then he swung his bolt cutters around like a golf club and he smashed them into the ball of my ankle.

The bathroom is cold.

The floor is soft underfoot and the mold is growing where the ceiling meets the walls. A web of mold like a fine mesh of lace. I flush the toilet. When I wash my hands the water is still boiling hot from the Rayburn stove. I look to the dark main room and the locked TV cabinet. Would I leave again now if I could? Would I jeopardize my sister's happiness, her future, her life? For what? What kind of life could I have now with this foot? At what moment did I reach that point of no return? These past years are stained indelibly onto my soul, engraved into my bones.

I sit on the lowest step of the staircase. There's a camera in here, too, one of seven. That day with the bolt cutters, that was my watershed. The voyage to the UK could have been a watershed and the job at the first farm with my sister could have been a watershed. But they weren't. What he did to me in his toolshed was my before and after. After he'd swung those bolt cutters I don't remember things very clearly. I think I passed in and out of consciousness, black to gray and back again. But I do remember him retelling me his rules while he twisted and manhandled my foot to ninety degrees. He retold me his rules as he pushed his weight down onto my foot and left me like this forever.

At school I ran the 400 meters. I wasn't the fastest, but I was a close second. That was a good distance for me. I wasn't explosive enough for the short sprints, nor stoic enough for long-distance. Four hundred meters was my race.

I reach up for the banister and pull myself up the stairs and go to bed.

6

On Christmas morning I don't wake until eleven. It's the one day a year Lenn takes off so it is the worst day of the whole year. He's here in his house all day long, apart from a brief break to feed his pigs. All internal doors open, no opportunity to discreetly read a page of my book or one of Kim-Ly's letters. No distance from him at all.

My head is foggy. It's been numb the past six weeks since he agreed to increase my dose to three-quarters of a horse pill per day. Vague. If you ask me what's happened in the past weeks I would tell you that nothing whatsoever has happened. Time has just moved on. The weather has been wet and still and nothing at all has happened.

"Happy Christmas, Jane," he says as I stop, panting, sweating, on the rough bottom step of the staircase. "I'll have me mug of tea and one of them mince pies in the next five minutes, please."

I go into the bathroom, door wide open, to wash. One of my back teeth is aching. My expression is that of a recently slaughtered animal. I have sleep crust in the corners of my eyes, and they're filmed with pink sludge. I pull my nightie over my head and don't look if he's there behind me watching or if he isn't. Chills run down my spine. An addict trapped inside a cage. I need a new pill but I'm sufficiently drowsy still, sufficiently embalmed, to not care about much. And yet, today, this seventh Christmas Day here in his house, is the day I have chosen to tell him.

The water from the faucet is lukewarm. I finish and dress and try to think of how I'll word it and what he'll say in response. What he'll *do* in response. My mouth tastes like I haven't brushed my teeth in weeks, and my right ankle is loose, the bones more fudgy than normal, more liable to snap away.

"There's your tea," I say to him, placing down his pesticide mug beside his armchair.

"Horse racin'," he says.

The TV is never on in the daytime, but this is Christmas. He's watching horse racing like a schoolboy, his socked feet pointing at the screen. I use his poker to spread the embers in the Rayburn, my hand gripping its iron handle, my arm less than four feet from his cranium, my head and my heart at odds, again. If I slay this man, my sister will have worked here for years and years in vain. If I do it I'd ruin her life for a singular moment of ecstasy. And anyway I know he'd intercept the poker. I tried to kill him years ago with a carving knife and he sensed what I was doing and blocked it with his arm. Hardly scratched him. I lost a bundle of handwritten letters from my mother that time.

I shove two knotty logs into the Rayburn and close the fire door shut.

"Pie," he says. "Mince pie."

I warm three mince pies, his mother's recipe, in the warming oven of the stove, and present them on his plate, and then I stand at the kitchen sink, my hands gripping the porcelain lip like a climber might cling to a granite ledge. The day is sodden. We've had cold

Christmases, even snow one year, but this is wet November weather cheating us on Christmas Day. I've missed the hour where the sun sits just above the horizon, beneath the clouds, above the earth, in the narrow strip we subsist in. I was comatose at that hour. Medicated with a horse pill. Outside, the drizzle is so fine it can't be seen, only felt.

I'll tell him later. It's the one day he's almost happy, the one day he has something other than the normal. An interruption of the usual food routine. Today we should be having ham, eggs, and fries. But we won't. This is the day I have selected to impart my private news. Something I've been in control of these past weeks. If he kills me then, according to his rules, Kim-Ly will be okay. There's that. If I kill myself, she'll be deported. If I kill him, she'll be deported, his friend Frank Trussock in the farm past the bridge will see to that. If I escape, she'll be deported. And she's so close. Eighteen months from now she'll be all paid up. Undocumented, of course, but paid up and free of the men who brought us here. She'll be living life. Her future will be in her hands and her hands only. And she'll be sending money, plenty of money back to Mom and Dad. By then they'll be desperate for it, if they're not already. I once thought of whether they were still alive, and then I made a pact with myself never to think of it again. Of course they are still alive. And on Fridays they drink beer together and eat peanuts. They still share that joy. If I start to imagine the alternative I clench my teeth and dig my fingernails into my palms and that forces the remainder of the thought to stay away.

"I'll get your pill, Jane."

He reaches up for the glass jar. These pills are pale blue and have a groove halfway across. He buys them from an agricultural dealer and there's never a label or a name or a logo or a list of possible side effects.

"Have that."

I swallow down the three-quarters of a pill. It's so large I can hardly do it because the edges of the tablet skirt my gullet and I can feel it work its way down into my stomach. By that point it's already starting to work and I'm light and I've pulled in tight within myself. My skin is ten times thicker than before and I'm hiding inside my own skeleton.

"Better get on with that bird if we are to eat before Boxin' Day."

He disappears into the bathroom and closes the door and locks it. I start peeling his potatoes. The turkey is a crown from the Spar shop. It's in its own little throwaway baking tray, so I just slide it into the Rayburn top oven and let it dry out nicely in there. Considering he's a farmer we eat like inner-city people. If we had a vegetable patch and a brood of chickens we'd live much better. Richer. I used to suggest it to him. I used to strive to enrich my miserable existence. To make the best of a very bad job. Not anymore. I'll eat the food from the Spar shop and I'll get through each day and I've stopped looking for better.

"*Raiders of the Lost Ark* in a bit," he says, rubbing his hands on his overalls as he emerges from the bathroom. "You seen it?"

I peel another potato, my hands dreamlike under the water, and I let the point of his mother's paring knife slip into my index finger. "No," I tell him, as a fine thread of blood swims and spirals and fans from just beneath my nail.

"Good'un," he says. "We'll watch it while the bird's cookin'."

I continue to prep the food. I didn't and don't feel any pain whatsoever from the cut to my finger. The pills are that good. I haven't run it under cold water and I haven't held it above my head the way my father taught me and I haven't wrapped it in paper towels. I'm just letting it bleed into his Christmas food.

"Come on," he says, patting the armrest of his chair.

I put the vegetables on top of the Rayburn hot plate to boil for hours and hours just the way he likes it, the way his mother did it, and then I sit down on the floor by his armchair.

He pats my hair.

I let my finger bleed into his floorboards.

It'll be me that cleans it all up later but I don't care. I pick at the cut and open it wide so that the blood can't coagulate and clot.

I focus on a spot between the top of the TV and the camera watching us. And I think of what's happening back at home right now. The food. The blessed warmth of the soil and the air. The vibrant colors. The flowers blooming in the brightest colors imaginable, brighter than the oilseed rape Lenn will grow next spring. Maybe my relatives have traveled into Saigon to visit a mall, buy small gifts for one another, go out for *bánh bèo*. They'll be laughing, chattering, patting each other's forearms and asking one another to pass the cucumber. They'll share their food. They'll smile.

When I stand up I almost fall over.

"You alright, Jane?"

"Fine," I say, lifting my right leg by the knee, gripping the back of his chair to help me over to the bathroom.

It hurts when I pee. The pills make this happen, they make me need to pee more often and they make it excruciatingly painful. My body is rotting from the inside at the constant fighting. The dependency. Animal medication polluting my human frame. I'll tell him today, I have to.

We eat at the pine table. He's placed two Christmas crackers from the Spar shop next to his mother's plates. He buys a box the week after Christmas and that box lasts us six years. He goes through this same tradition every year. No tree, no decorations, no gifts, no songs, no cards. But always two Spar crackers.

"Ain't bad," he says, shoveling turkey breast and roast potato and cabbage onto his fork. "Maybe more time in the oven next year, eh?"

Next year. Will I still be here next year? How can I be?

I nod.

I eat it and it tastes as bland as the Sunday roast chicken I cook for him every weekend. There is literally no difference between that dry bird and this one. With the same carcass I could make him a rich, fragrant *phở* broth, layered with noodles and peppercorns and mint and coriander and chilies and green onions. But he will not allow it. In the early days I would plead for him to let me cook it for myself at least, just for lunch. The ingredients are cheap. But he would say, *You got to eat English now, Jane, you live here in England now.*

He pushes the red cracker at me.

I grip it.

He pulls his end while maintaining eye contact. Those dead fish eyes of his. He pulls gently and looks at me and then the cracker separates and goes bang and he smiles and pulls out his hat and his joke and his toy.

"Mini screwdrivers," he says. Then he puts his hat on. It's blue. He reads the joke and smiles but doesn't share it.

I stretch my cracker out to him and we go through the same thing again. I win. The toy is a key ring. The joke is the same joke I had five years ago. I put on the hat. Lime green. He takes the key ring from me. "I'll have that, might come in useful, that might."

We sit with the Rayburn door open. There's a small cardboard box of Quality Street chocolates on his knee. He likes them. All except the strawberry ones and the orange ones. He drops those on the floor by my mangled foot.

"Nothin' on TV, never is," he says. "Not like the old days, Morecambe and Wise. Me mother used to howl at them, she did."

He says all this every Christmas but never does anything about it.

"Load of rubbish, really," he says. "Not worth paying the license fee."

He switches off the TV and drops another strawberry cream by my sandal, his sandal.

"Why don't you run a good hot bath," he says.

The hairs on my arms stand on end and the chill from the windows and the walls and that uneven bathroom floor creeps up my shins. I move away from the armchair and collect up the wrappers that I'd arranged on the blood spatter from my fingertip, and stand, unsteadily, and throw them into the Rayburn fire. The flames crackle and leap as they engulf the red and orange plastic wrappers. I watch them shrivel to nothing. Turn to heat and smoke. The glare hurts my eyes and I step over to the pine table.

"Lenn, I've got something to tell you."

"Somethin' to tell me?"

"I think—"

"You don't tell me nothin' less I ask you to. Now, get in the bathroom and run a hot bath."

"Lenn."

He looks up at me, a toffee candy visible on the flat of his tongue.

"I'm pregnant."

"You're what?"

We look at each other. He takes the toffee candy out of his mouth and I hold on to the table for support.

"How?"

I shrug.

"I don't do nothin' inside you. Nothin'."

I know.

"I used me towel."

I know.

"Did you plan this, did you?"

What?

He stands up and storms out of the room, grabbing his jacket as he leaves through the front door. He stumbles putting on his boots. The TV cabinet's unlocked, it's the first time he's left it unlocked. I watch him out the window as he stomps off toward his quad, his blue cracker hat still on his head. He's going to feed his pigs.

I know I should be thinking about this baby but really it's too small to think about. Too ridiculous. I can't even feel it. My breasts are sore, they're fuller, and my skin feels different, but I can't think of this thing as a baby. And anyway, it's his. What monster will this child grow into? What demon? I can't be responsible for the continuation of the bloodline. That would be a crime. For the past weeks, since I missed my period, since I figured out what must have happened, I've worried about this child growing into an adult. Looking like him. Being like him.

But it's me I need to think of now. For nine months I will have to sleep with him in his front bedroom, in his bed. No six days off a month in the small back bedroom. No escape from him asking me to take a bath. I will have nine months with no distance from this.

I've thought about killing it but I have no idea how. Maybe if I didn't take one of the pills, if I coughed it up, did that several times. Could I take an overdose of these farm tablets, these veterinary drugs? It'd kill the baby, surely. Or maybe it would just hurt us both. Make us sick.

I will the baby gone. If I don't want it, if I tell myself it's just him, a smaller version of him, a vile copy, my body might expel it. It might. I have no connection to this child, no attachment, no love. I want it gone.

What now?

How do I manage all this? With my ankle?

I sit down on the plastic-wrapped sofa and reach into his box of Quality Street and take a green triangle, praline, his favorite, and unwrap it, and let it melt on my tongue.

7

I missed Valentine's Day.

In years gone by I would glance at the Massey Ferguson flip calendar on the wall, the one next to the kitchen sink window, the one
I hang up on the same brass thumbtack each January. If I removed
that calendar right now, I'd find seven holes. They'd look like bullet
holes on some minuscule firing range, all close together, a cluster
marking how long I've been here, how long I've been attaching his
farming calendars to his wall. But now I chart time differently. It's
nothing to do with him, nothing he's part of. My diary, my calendar,
my watch: it's all inside my body.

I'm starting to show.

I'm not having any particular issues with my back or my clothes,
her clothes. But I can feel it. Him, her, it. I don't trust it but I do love
it. How did that happen? From hatred and fear to love. Already.
I think of this tiny thing often, all the time, every waking hour. I
hated it for a while and then, all of a sudden, I accepted it.

This baby will be mine, not his.

"Get the kettle on. I'm freezin' me hands off out there."

I take the cast-iron kettle from the Rayburn and fill it from the faucet and open the lid to the hot plate and place it down. The drips on the bottom hiss and roll around the hot surface and then they're gone.

Lenn's covered in paint. He's wearing his new overalls, got them from the farm supplies catalog, the one I still read when I can get access to it away from a camera, hungry for new information, new language, new images. The Argos catalog served me well for years. It taught me so much. I found comfort in its pages, its index, its photographs, in the subtle differences between the thousands of products. But that was before.

"Old plow's about had it," he says, staring out the window toward the track and the locked halfway gate and the road beyond. "Maybe get another year out of it if we're lucky."

I give him his pesticide mug of sweet beige tea.

"You want me to tidy your toolshed?" I ask. "I'm done in here."

He looks at me and looks down at my belly. "Don't hide nothin' in there or play daft games, don't move nothin'."

I nod and he hands me his empty mug, blue paint bordering his nails and his bloodied cuticles.

Since Christmas I've thought about the woman who visited, the one who wanted a field for her horse. I try to remember her name but I just can't. My brain is addled. Soft. Imprecise. She had red hair and she smiled with all of her features, I remember that.

Last night Lenn told me about his camper holidays, the ones he had as a child with his mother. He tells me about them more often since he found out about the baby. Not in any great detail, no sentimentality, just where they went and for how long. Logistics rather than emotion. Crabbing. Cotton candy. Rock candy made from sugar with words running through it. I still can't picture it but I try. Piers with arcades. Kites. I can tell they're his favorite memories. He clings to them. Perhaps they were the days when he got away, when his mother, Jane, let him escape this bleakest of all fenland farms.

I rest my foot. It throbs and stabs me in the eyes with its pain, but I need to rest it and the pills are starting to fail me. I want more. I want full pills, the whole thing, no ends chipped off. My body craves them but I think the baby does as well. We need more. It'll mess up my system in other ways, I know that, but I want more medication. And, also, I don't. Because the more I take the more I need him and the more he can do whatever he wants to me and the greater risk there will be to the baby and, most terrifying of all, the more I'll resist ever trying to leave. Or rather, the less energy I'll devote to figuring out something smart, a plan where my sister is safe and I get to leave this place once and for all. But I can hardly sew a button or set the washing machine these days, my brain's so muddy. I went a whole week last month without thinking one proper complete thought.

I get up and go outside.

It's the only respite I get from his cameras. There is no back bedroom time anymore, only him on top of that damn sheet and me underneath it. Night after night.

The day is clear and the sky is as blue as glacial meltwater. He's painting the sprayer now up by the locked halfway gate. I hobble around the outside of the house, my hand on the wall to keep my weight off my ankle. The ground's hard now. Dead grass and no insects. The spires are there like upturned nails on the edge of the world, each one a signal, a symbol, a finger pointing out and saying *I'm here, come to safety* and I see them every day and I can't reach them. One would be infuriating but being able to see seven separate parish churches is some kind of mean-spirited joke.

I reach out and let my fingertip follow the smooth curved edge of a yellow hard candy. It might crack in the cold nights but so far it's alright. I've been hiding more since Christmas, since I told Lenn about the baby. I might need them. The sugar might come in useful for the grueling days to come.

His shed is already tidy, old wooden tools hanging from their hooks, a bucket of oily sand ready and waiting in the corner for rinsed spades and forks to be dipped into, the jagged crystals cleaning them back to pure steel, the oil coating them until the next use. Lenn takes care of his tools.

The bolt cutters are here. Always here. Reminding me. They lie horizontally at the end wall resting on two six-inch nails. They taunt me. There is no handcuff keeping me here, there is no manacle locked around my ankle. And yet I am imprisoned.

I sweep the floor with his broom, pushing wood shavings out into the cold, dry air. The fringe of grass poking in from outside is yellow. I pull out my book from my apron, his mother's apron, and read. It's the section where Lennie hides a mouse in his pocket. A dead mouse. It's the part where George discovers it and takes it from him. I reach down and place a hand on my bump. It's hard. The baby doesn't move. Maybe that will come later. But I worry the baby doesn't move because of the drugs, and living here, the wretched food he buys from the Spar shop in the village, the lack of nutrition, the lack of joy in my life.

Right now it's *Tét*, the Vietnamese Lunar New Year. My seventh here, my ninth in this country. More important for us than Christmas. A time of heat and humidity and red dragons and feasting and coming together for a few days. The *Tét* celebrations I experienced on the first farm were grim, but they were everything compared to this. Kim-Ly and I would save from the cash pay packet envelopes we received every Friday. We'd get what ingredients we could from a Tesco nearby on the edge of town. One year we found mung bean puree next to the lentils and the boil-in-the-bag rice and we both cried with laughter. Delight. Relief. We cooked the dishes, less than half of what we'd have prepared back home, and shared *bánh chưng,* sticky rice parcels, with our Polish and Romanian housemates. They enjoyed them, they really did. At the time they tasted strange and they were not good enough but looking back from this flat fen I think of those meals as state banquets. Nine of us living in a house built for two, mattresses arranged on the floor, people sitting cross-legged, steaming bowls of food between us, cans of Coke and bottles of beer. The Poles and the Romanians were kind to us. They were fair. I haven't had a proper drink since the day I left that first farm. Lenn's mother didn't drink so neither does Lenn.

The house is cool when I get back inside, so I stoke up the Rayburn with coppiced willow and I take a rest on the bed upstairs. He lets me rest for half an hour in the daytime on account of the "young'un." I lie with my hands on my child, on my stomach, my hard, ever-changing lower-belly. What will become of this unmoving little person? How will I bring it into this world, this place; how will I care for it? I've asked Lenn about seeing a doctor or a midwife and he said *Ain't likely.* I asked him about diapers and a crib, about baby clothes, about the things I know or think I know this child will need. He ignores my questions. My pills make my head throb but they help my ankle. It's a perilous balancing act. When I have ten minutes left of my rest break I fall into a deep sleep, and then I wake up and the clock says ten to five. I scramble, panicking, across to the banister and, holding it tight in my armpit, inching down the stairs as if descending some mountain pass, I make it to the bottom just before he arrives in the entrance hall and takes off his blue-marked overalls and boots and his wool hat.

"I can't smell no pie? Somethin' wrong?"

"I've stoked up the fire, it'll be ready soon."

He goes into the bathroom and closes the door behind him.

I take the pie from the fridge, which I made last night with leftovers from the dry roast chicken, and place it as high as possible in the main oven of the Rayburn. I fill the firebox with wood and open the vents and blow to get the fire going.

Lenn walks back in and sits at the computer to review the tapes.

"You didn't clean that sink proper," he says. "Mother used to bleach it every day, scrub it after."

"Okay," I say.

"Hang on."

I check the pie in the oven, some impulse telling me the smell of it cooking might appease him.

"How long did you put your feet up for, then?"

I look at him.

"You do that again and I'll have your letters, alright? This ain't no bleedin' holiday camp. Me mother used to work her fingers to the bone out here and then you come, rent free, not a care in the world, waltzed right into this country, into this house, and just lay about." He turns and looks straight at me. "I won't have it, Jane."

My name is not Jane.

"I'm off to feed the pigs, have me pie on the table by the time I get back in."

I check on the pie when he's gone and it's warming up, the pastry browning, but the insides are probably still cool. He took my ID card last month. I'd forgotten to set out his towel, the small one he uses after he makes me have a bath. I'd not taken it out of the linen closet or placed it on his side of the bed, and when it came time for him to finish, he'd groaned a different groan than normal. Like he was in pain without that towel. And then he took me downstairs and he made me put my three remaining possessions on the plastic-wrapped sofa and made me pick one, and now I'm afraid that if things keep going on like this I'll forget my real name, my birthday, my place of birth, and I won't have my ID card to remind me.

There's a light out front.

I hobble to the window and wipe the condensation with my hand. It's a truck up by the locked halfway gate. I open the front door and the chilly air cools my arms and sends my hairs standing up and my flesh all bumped.

It's a fire truck.

Men are getting out of the cab at the front.

I step outside.

They're shouting something but I can't hear them.

They're in uniform, official uniforms: hats, reflective jackets, boots.

There are three or four of them. Walking toward me. I hold out my hand and then their voices get drowned out by the screaming engine of Lenn's quad as he races up to meet them. I watch them talk. They look over at me and one of them shakes Lenn's hand and then they climb back into their fire truck and turn and drive away.

8

It's Easter weekend and he's planting oilseed rape. He says it's his most important crop of the year.

I've been helping Lenn with the farm paperwork: subsidy forms and reordering. I'm better with numbers than he is and it keeps him off my back. He expects me to scrub and clean and cook the same as I always do, but with my bump, and my back as bad as it is, and my ankle more swollen than ever, I need to sit down more. I use the desktop PC, him watching me.

The skies are at their most interesting this time of year. The colors but also the depth. Swirls and wafers and false worlds. Layers of cloud like sedimentary rock strata built up over the ages. Earlier this morning everything above soil level was rose pink.

"Get them fries on," says Lenn as he walks in, the doorframe behind him twilight gray. "And don't dry them eggs too hard, keep them yellas runny."

He sits down to review the day's tapes as I get the McCain fries out of the freezer.

"You know what you said about that woman," I say.

He grunts and keeps his watery eyes on the screen.

"For the baby."

"What you talkin' about?"

"The woman. You said—"

"Ain't no woman needed, changed me mind. Ain't nothing I can't do myself." He looks over at me. "Get them fries in that stove and come here."

I do it.

"Get them films up."

"Which films?"

He moves aside and I sit down at the PC.

"All them you showed me. Short films. When I fixed the washin' machine that time. Them videos tellin' you how to fix this thing and that."

"YouTube?"

"That's it."

I google YouTube, and because our internet's so damn slow the homepage takes minutes to load. The smell of hot oil starts to fill the room.

"When it comin' out of you?"

I touch my stomach.

He looks down and says, "When's he comin' out, Jane?"

"Soon."

"Get a video up on how to do it. Me mother did it with me, mothers have been doin' it for thousands of years, can't be nothin' to it. Find a good video and get on with them eggs."

"But you said you know a woman." He looks agitated. "Please, Lenn. We need proper help."

"You get a video up or else we won't know nothin', will we? Find a good'un."

I search for DIY home births and wait for the results.

"That's them," he says.

I select one and click on it.

"That's it," he says.

I vacate the chair and start to fry ham and eggs on the top of the Rayburn in his mother's cast-iron skillet. The oil spits and burns my wrist and I watch it redden and I let it.

"Film's not workin'," he says. "Ah, it's comin' now."

I can't watch.

I stand at the stove, the heat from the fire warming my bump, and watch the egg whites bubble and shake.

Screams pour out of the computer.

Lenn's entranced; he has his head close to the monitor, his hands gripping the table.

A large bubble develops on one of the egg whites so I pop it with his mother's spatula and it deflates and sinks and sizzles in the oil. The screams change. It's a baby screaming now and the mother is quiet. My shoulders ease. Lenn's just watched a baby being born and that one seems to have turned out alright.

"Bleedin' hell," he says.

I flip the eggs gently and slide them from the pan onto the plates, three for him and two for me. Ham. I take the fries from the oven and shake them and arrange them the way he likes and place both plates down on the table and pour lime juice for us both.

"It's alright," he says, plunging his knife into a runny yolk. "I knew it'd be nothin' much. I can do it."

You can do it?

"But if something goes wrong?" I say. "If there's a complication?"

He chews his ham and eggs and there's a sliver of oil shining from his clean-shaven chin.

"If it mucks up, we'll see to it then. Play it by ear."

I eat and the baby kicks. A protest.

I thought of a good name for him or her the other day, a good strong name, but now I can't remember it.

"You don't remember nothin', do you?"

"Sorry?"

"Of the early days, you don't remember nothin' what happened, do you?"

"I do."

"You don't. Where did I take you on our honeymoon?"

I look down at my dinner.

"You remember it?"

I look at him.

"Was Skeggy, you remember? Two nights. You loved it."

"Honeymoon?"

I do recall a beach. Being so sedated I could hardly walk. I'm not sure if I was there for an hour or a weekend.

"You don't remember much from the good old days, do you, with that head of yours?"

"Good old days?"

It's not the drugs causing me to misremember. There weren't any good old days, not with you, not ever, not one single good old day.

He stands up and pushes his chair back and the legs squeak on the floor.

I don't like this. Because he's not finished his dinner and he's breaking his routines. He never does this.

I hear him approach the door to the half-cellar, the door immediately facing his front door. I've never been down there because that was a rule from day one. Also, because it smells awful, or it did the first year I was here, rotten meat and old bins, decay, and because it's half height, you can't stand up straight, not even close, and because there are no stairs, just a steep ladder. He unbolts the upper bolt and then he unbolts the lower bolt. He switches the light on down there. I can see a dim glow by my feet from between the floorboards. He comes back up.

"Found it."

He hands me a piece of cardboard. I take it from him and flip it over and it's a bent frame with a photo in the center. Me and him. Mold spores on the edges of the frame. Me in a white wedding dress and a veil. Spots of damp on the image. A vacant expression on my face. The remnants of a cobweb on the cardboard. Him in a shirt and tie.

"Remember it now, do you?"

I say nothing.

What is this?

"I'll find honeymoon snaps one day and all, some good'uns of you on Skeggy Beach. Right windy it was. Gusty."

I start to ask a question and then swallow the word.

"We gonna be a family after this, Jane. The three of us here in me mother's old cottage. I ain't gonna let nothin' bad happen to the young'un when he comes out, you don't need to worry yourself on that front."

"Can I see a doctor?"

He takes the photo back from me.

"We'll see, that's all I'm sayin'. Watched a video just now, a good'un. I think I can do it, bring that young'un out of you with no bother. You're strong, you'll be fine. Me mother was alright here with nobody about. I'll give you a full pill when it starts to come out, full pain pill if you need it."

This is the most we've spoken in years. I point to the photo.

"Are you saying that I wanted to marry you?"

He points to my smiling face in the photo.

"I want to be with my sister when the baby comes, Lenn," I say. "I want to be with her."

"Wait there."

He goes back down to the half-cellar and I can sense his bulk underneath me. I can hear him rummage, he must be bent double, and I can see the light from down there through the gaps in the rough timber floorboards. He comes back up.

"Found it."

He hands me a wedding veil. It's gray and the edges have been gnawed at by mice, but it's lace and it's beautiful and I can't recall ever seeing it before apart from ten minutes ago in that photograph. I was either too comatose or else I've deleted the memory.

I look up at the camera in the corner of the room.

He follows my gaze.

"Filmin's for your own good, see, and it'll be safer having the cameras now with the young'un coming. What with your bad leg, needed to see you were alright, you weren't havin' no bother. Havin' cameras is the same as that YouTube you showed me on the computer, same thing."

"Lenn, I want to be with Kim-Ly for the birth. I'll come back, I promise you. Can you let me be with her just for the birth?"

"Ain't nothing she can do for you that I can't."

Tears form somewhere in my eyes but nothing comes to the surface. I lost all hope years ago and this is just fresh misery.

"I'll put these back in the cellar and go feed the pigs. Why don't you run yourself a good full bath while the stove's hot."

He leaves. As I collect the plates and glasses and cutlery from the table, I see lights up the track. There's a small car by the locked halfway gate. I set down the plates and stagger to the front door. Can't fall now, not like this, not with the bump so big, can't hurt it.

There's a figure walking toward the house.

Lenn's at the back of the house, he's feeding the pigs. He'll be gone awhile, he might not have seen the car.

It's her, the woman with the red hair and horsey jodhpurs. What was her name?

I step to the door so the camera can't see me but I keep my right foot out of sight.

"Hope you don't mind me dropping in again," she says. "You're not in the middle of dinner or anything, are you?"

I shake my head and I want to tell her everything.

"Look at you," she says, a broad smile on her lips, a new shade of lipstick, dark pink. She's pointing to my belly. "Congratulations, Jane. How many months are you?"

My name is not Jane.

"About seven," I say.

"Do you know the sex?"

She's not nosy, just naturally friendly, her face says she's delighted for me, she sees me as some sort of friend, some sort of neighbor.

I shake my head. "We didn't want to know."

My throat closes up with this lie. This cover-up.

"So exciting!"

She wears a cross on a necklace.

"Could you post a letter for me?" I ask.

She frowns and then laughs, her red hair moving in front of her eyes.

"I can if you like, but you shouldn't stop going out, you know. My sister had awful back trouble, bad morning sickness at the start, really tough final trimester, but she got out and about as much as she could. Shopping and walking in the fields. Of course, we're all different. But the first few days after you get back from the hospital you'll be locked away in here so make the most of the freedom while you have it."

The freedom while I have it.

"Are you a midwife?" I ask. "A nurse?"

She laughs.

"I'm just a photographer," she says, zipping up her fleece jacket. "Portraits, headshots, that kind of thing. Although I've started doing landscapes since moving here. These skies!"

I want to tell her.

I want for her to call the police. She'll have a cell phone with her, everyone does.

I want for her to put me in her car and take me straight to Manchester to see Kim-Ly.

"Anyway, I just wondered if your husband was around? Or maybe you've spoken with him? About the field. I'll be buying a horse this summer so I'm really keen to rent something and your land would be perfect, just an acre or two."

I want to tell her but I can't. My insides are screaming, *Let her help you, do not let go of this lifeline, be smart.*

But what would he do to the baby if he caught me?

"He's busy with the pigs," I say. "Could you come back next month when he'll have finalized his plans and he'll be able to decide then?"

I want her to come back. I want to save Kim-Ly. But I really want her to come back one day when I've worked out how to do this. How to save us both, me and the baby.

She looks down at my left foot. I'm wearing Lenn's old sandals, size eleven. She looks into the house.

"Is everything alright, Jane?"

"I'm sorry," I say. "I've forgotten your name."

"Cynthia," she says. "Call me Cynth, everyone does."

And then I realize she's looking at my right foot, at its reflection in the entrance mirror.

I close the door a fraction.

"I'll tell Lenn you stopped by," I say, closing the door more. "Come back next month and we'll see what we can do."

Two weeks ago he withheld my medication.

He found out about Cynthia. Cynth. I must remember her name. I must cling to it and carve it into my memory. He could see Cynth on the tapes and although I told him I didn't say anything, although he could see that for himself, see that I closed the door on her, he locked the horse pills down in the half-cellar for three whole days.

The pain almost ended me.

The pain of my ankle under all this new weight, but even more, the pain of not having the horse pills when I expect them, when my body expects them. The lack of that surge, that assistance, that sweet, essential numbness.

On the first night I slept on the floor with my ankle held against the cold wall and my back arched like some dark folkloristic creature hiding in the forest. I wailed without noise.

When he brought the glass bottle back up from the half-cellar, from his half-cellar, he offered me a whole pill and told me I'd learned my lesson and I looked into his eyes and, through gritted teeth, I told him I'd just take half. Those three days of agony were the price I paid for lucidity. I will need my mind clear for the months ahead. To protect my baby and myself and to watch out for him and also so I'll remember. Most of my life here I want to forget, that's what I am looking for, to create some space between the core me and this so-called life. But the birth. My first. Probably also my last. I need to be clearheaded. I'll take medication to dull the pain, I'm no hero, no superwoman. But I want to see my baby's face, to really *see* it.

So now I'm on half a pill each day and I can tolerate the pain just about. Mostly. Every time the bone shards in my ankle joint—if you can call it a joint, there's nothing much joined-up inside there—scrape together and the darts and needles stab up my back, up my neck, each time the pain drags the breath from my lungs, I touch my belly. I started out hating this living thing, hating it growing inside me, because it's his and because I had no conscious or willing role in its creation. But then, over time, with it moving and kicking and me being able to tell which way it's lying inside of me, I have grown to love it as if I've known it for a hundred lifetimes. I speak to it. We talk without words. We make plans together but my child will never be the George to my Lennie or the Lennie to my George. I speak and try to whisper Vietnamese nursery rhymes and Steinbeck's words and I try to sound strong and able and reassuring. Like a mother.

Right now I'm painting the bathroom. The mold spores have spread across the ceiling and they're making the room smell worse than ever and I fear for this baby. It hasn't breathed its first breath yet and I worry for its olive-size lungs and its future here with Lenn as its father.

But Lenn is not its father, not since the moment after conception, because I have claimed this baby as my own. I will be mother and father. I will be extended family, aunts, and uncles. I will be my own mother and father, the good teachers I had, the wise friends. I pledge to be these people to this child because all it has is me.

The chemical paint smell makes me retch. He bought it from the town past the bridge. When he left he'd said he'd be about an hour but he was back within ten minutes looking at me through the window, his rough hands cupped to the glass. Checking on me. Now that I'm a month away, maybe six weeks, he's paranoid I'll leave. He's more paranoid than ever. How could I leave? Even if I decided to effectively send Kim-Ly back, to ruin her life, to make her years of secret labor count for nothing, even if I did make that heartless decision, how could I leave? I can't even walk out of here when I'm not pregnant, I'd surely lie down and perish by the halfway gate if I tried it now.

I dab his brush into his tin of paint and cover his mold. It takes two thick coats of rubbery white paint and it will still grow back, somehow it's guaranteed not to, I read on the tin. I read any text I can get my hands on; I used to read the Argos catalog every day until he found out and burned it in the Rayburn.

In years gone by I would paint and clean and cook for him, but now I do it for my child. I used to sleep and wash and comb my hair for him, but now I do it all for my child. My child.

Cynth hasn't come back.

I apply the paint, and hairs from the old brush fall out and lie entombed in the thick white liquid, and I dream of Cynth arriving with the police, offering some kind of unheard-of immigration immunity for Kim-Ly, a team of kind, decent people swooping in, all because she gleaned from the reflection of my right ankle in the hallway mirror all that I have been through and am still going through.

I visualize my baby's nursery every night before falling asleep. Not the actual nursery, which is one rattle I found in the storage closet, his mother's rattle bought for Lenn, but my dream nursery. From the 2004 Argos catalog. A pine crib and a black car seat with a secure belt. A soft blanket that no other being has used before. And a big pack of disposable diapers, wet wipes, bottles, a sterilization machine. I remember the machines vividly: four different makes and models to choose from. The baby would have a range of one-sies, some hats and mittens, a bouncy chair, perhaps a pacifier. But, in reality, it just has me and Lenn's old rattle. I will have to be all of those other things. I will have to be its nursery.

I hear the front door.

"Cheese sandwich," says Lenn from the main room. "Mug of tea, no juice."

I drop the brush into the paint tin and grip the dry part of the wall and climb awkwardly down the small stepladder, taking my time over each narrow rung.

"Been sprayin', wind's picking up down by the big barley field, muckin' it up."

I wash my hands with scalding-hot water and then I make his lunch and I make mine.

"Been thinking about names," he says as he chews his Mighty White cheese sandwich.

Nothing to do with you, Lenn.

"Been thinking about Jeff or Gordon." He takes a swig of luke-warm beige sweet tea. "Jeff was me granddad and Gordon was me mother's sister's husband, good lad was Gordon, strong as a bull."

It's not your child, Lenn. Not anymore. Nothing whatsoever to do with you.

"I reckon Jeff," he says.

I finish painting the bathroom ceiling and then, after chicken broth made from yesterday's discount Spar shop bird, we watch *Match of the Day*. He insists I still sit on the floor even though he needs to help me up. The wooden boards are cold and the draft from the half-cellar below is stale and sour.

"Best time of day, ain't it?" he says. "Nothin' wrong with a bit of TV together after a hard day's work. Not a bad life here, is it, Jane?"

I block him out. I'm stroking the head of my child inches beneath my own skin and I'm dreaming up childhoods for it. Plural. Different potential futures, with stepdads, with me and my parents, with Kim-Ly in Manchester.

Before the birth I'll prepare the small back bedroom as best I can. I'll have to use pillows on the bed to create a makeshift crib for when I need to do my chores and the baby's sleeping. Lenn's told me I'll be getting two days off like his mother had with him and then full resumption of normal service, no lying about. He says it's not healthy for a woman.

"Manchester United, your favorite," he says.

And then the baby kicks me but it feels different.

My attention, every joule of energy I have is focused on my womb. Inside my womb. My baby. It's moving and it doesn't feel right.

"Lenn," I say. "The baby."

"What?"

"It doesn't feel right. It's too early, too small."

"What do you mean?"

He stands up and looks down at me.

"It's okay," I say. "I think it's back to normal. I think. But, Lenn. You said you know of a woman. Who could come here. Who wouldn't say a word."

"I told you before, there ain't no woman."

"But if there's a problem? Because of the pills or something?"

"If it ain't meant to live it'll end up in the dike just like me brother did."

The blood inside my veins freezes to ice. I stiffen at his words.

"No."

I wouldn't let him.

"Your brother?"

I reach up to the sofa armrest to pull myself up and Lenn helps me to sit on it.

"Passed on when I was seven and he was the size of a cookin' apple. Not enough time in the oven me mother said. Poor little thing."

"You know I could die, Lenn. During childbirth. So could the baby."

"We'll see. I watched the video on the computer. I know what I'm doin', I ain't thick."

"I'm sorry about your brother."

"Happens out here. Just happens. You got to get on with it."

I stay seated on the sofa and Lenn adds a couple of logs to the Rayburn—we don't need as much this time of year—and sits back down.

The evening light is warm and the shadow of the house is as long as a field. Out the kitchen window I can see the pig barn in the distance, its cinder-block walls and corrugated-iron roof glowing like a gemstone.

"That weren't a goal, that were offside, did you see that, Jane?"

I need the bathroom. It stinks of chemical stain-blocker paint and I sit there with the door wide open and the TV flickering from the main room. Kim-Ly's last letter is still fresh in my head and I can read her writing line by line in my mind again now that I've cut back to half a horse pill a day. Her handwriting is more fluid than my own, more alive. Her grades were always better than mine. Especially mathematics and science. She told me in the letter how her job was raided by the border control people two weeks before and she'd had to run out of the fire exit and hide down a side street until it was safe, between a brick wall and a dumpster. She couldn't even go back to her apartment because they raided that too. But she keeps her ID card and passport in the attic and they didn't think to look there. She's okay. Kim-Ly works six days per week and has four repeat customers that she really likes. They ask her things. Like her actual name. They're interested in what she has to say, they really listen to her answers. But then there are the other customers, the women who come in before a night out, stressed, in a hurry, looking at their phones. She wrote that she doesn't mind these women if they're not regulars, but some of them see her every week and treat her like a vending machine or a parking meter.

I stand up to flush and there's blood in the water.

My breathing quickens and I wrap my hands around my bump and slow my heart so I can hear it, feel it, check on it.

He shouts "lime juice" from the main room.

The blood is new, fresh, light in color, pinkish. I talk to the baby silently without using my lips. I ask it, *Are you okay?*

And then there's something warm on my leg.

My water has broken.

10

I don't say a word.

This is a moment for myself. A moment I own. A moment to register what is happening. This moment is for me and my child.

I look at my bare legs, at the puddle by the base of the toilet.

"Starting, is it?" he says, right behind me, in the doorway, looking at the floor, looking at me, uninvited.

I nod.

"Early, is it?" he says.

"Too early," I say. "Lenn, it's too small. I need some help."

"Be back in a bit," he says, turning and leaving.

I clean up the clear fluid and flush the toilet and sit on the plastic dust sheet of the sofa. The air is warm. I'm cramping but I've had no contractions, at least I don't think I have. I'll soon need the toilet again.

By the time Lenn gets back, my contractions are ten minutes apart and I know exactly what they feel like.

"Get off the settee, Jane," he says. "I'll set you up next to the table."

He unfolds a green tarp—something you'd use to cover a hole in a roof—and flattens it down on the floor opposite the Rayburn. It's covered in leaves and dry dirt.

I look at it and look at him.

"I'll brush the muck off."

"I need the bathroom."

"It's alright as long as you keep the door open."

"No, I mean I need help walking there."

He swallows and I see his Adam's apple roll down beneath his collar and up again. He helps me up and then supports me to the bathroom. The pain is intensifying and I wonder at what point, if at all, this will overtake my ankle pain. Will the two run concurrently or will one eclipse the other?

"Don't go making a big deal about all this, not a mother on the planet who ain't been through all this, don't go making a big fuss about it."

I want to gouge his eyes out with a pencil.

He helps me to the tarp and I rest with my back against the wall. In front of me is the stove, to the left of me is the kitchen, to the right of me is the locked TV cabinet and the camera and the window.

"Get the pills down off the shelf," I say.

"You've had your half, had it with your cornflakes. I watched it."

I clench my teeth through a contraction. When it's passed I say, "Get the pills down now."

He stretches for the jar and unscrews the lid.

"How many?"

"Two," I say. "Break them up into pieces."

He does it.

I'm not in full labor yet and the contractions are small. I need the pill fragments lined up now because I can't be negotiating with him later on, I don't want to have to speak with him at all later on. That time's for me and my child. It'll need me and I'll need it, we live as one today or we die as one.

"Like having a lamb, me mother used to say, same difference."

Shut. Your. Mouth.

"Me granddad had lambs for a time. Up inland he was, small farm, rocky land and no good drainage. Went up there as a lad." My contraction kicks in and my back stiffens and the pain is like a solid object. "Saw lambin' as a lad, nothing to it really, slipped out they did, some had three young'uns and most of them survived good into summer."

I take a fragment of a pill, maybe a fifth, and swallow it dry.

"Water," I say.

He huffs and pours me a glass of water and leaves it by my hand.

"Want the TV on?" he says.

I close my eyes tight. If my sister were here, what would she do? She'd have me in bed, not on some dirty tarp. She'd have fresh towels and baby clothes at the ready, pain medication and hot water and pressed linen. She'd have a bowl of fruit: some candied, some fresh.

The next contraction comes at me like a wave I never saw. My God. It's like my womb is pulling itself apart, the pressure deep down, way down, spreading my skeleton, moving the bones that took a lifetime to form. I scream out and pant like an animal.

He comes to me. He looks down disapprovingly and removes his belt. I recoil. What is this? What is he doing?

He bends it, looping it over on itself, the cracked brown leather splitting at each traverse.

"Bite down on it if you need to, Jane."

What century am I trapped in?

He hands it to me and I place it down by my bad foot.

The hour hand drags itself around the clockface and the baby does not come out of me. Hours of pain. The contractions are closer, they're harder. I've had one and a third horse pills on top of my usual half and my head is awash with dreamlike images and thick fog. There's blood on the tarp. It pooled by my legs and my ankles and he didn't clean it up. It's dried now, stuck to some oak leaves and wheat husks, dried into some unheard-of fertility emblem from a different place and a different time. I can't focus. The things I see at the edges of my eyes are hazy and when the pains come, as spaced-out and regular as the heartbeat of a blue whale deep underwater, my eyes fog completely and I throw back my head and I sob.

My ankle is nothing.

The pains aren't eclipsing, they aren't concurrent, they are different. Separate, but together. The pills help but I'm weak now. Exhausted. How do women do this with no pain relief? Why do they do it?

"I need food," I say to him.

He looks over from the armchair, the blue clock of *Countdown* on the TV, and says, "Cheese and ham?"

I nod.

I feel sick, I can't eat, but I can't afford to pass out either.

He makes sandwiches for both of us.

I wail as the next contraction strikes me. It's a period cramp amplified to the point where I'm breaking apart. Cracking open. I feel down for the baby's head between my legs but there's nothing. How long can I do this?

"Have your sandwich, then," he says. "Made it for you so eat it up, do you some good."

I eat it because I really need the fuel, and then, during the lull between the pains, I throw it back up.

"That's why I brought the tarp in, you see that now, don't you?" He throws me a roll of paper towels. "For your mess, that is."

"I need the bathroom."

"Again?" he asks.

"Help me up."

I try to go but I can't. Nothing. But the sitting down on the toilet is more comfortable for now. It's better than the floor.

"Can you help me up to bed?" I say.

"Nobody's havin' no young'un upstairs. Got you all set up down here, don't go makin' no fuss, it's what you women been doing hundreds of years. Me mother had me down here, right in this spot, it's the best place for it."

He helps me back to the tarp and I squat for a while and take the belt between my teeth and bite down so hard during a contraction that my teeth move in my gum sockets. The leather tastes of him and it tastes of cow.

"It's alright," I say to the baby, whisper to it, "you're doing well."

Lenn shakes his head. "Daft."

There are more contractions and more pill fragments. Lenn throws a pile of newspapers down on the floor. I have no idea what they're for.

"Need to get sprayin' before too long, wind gonna pick up, or so the radio said."

I want him to leave me here but it's the wrong thing to want. I may need him. I want this to be me and the baby, nothing connected with him whatsoever, but what if there's a problem, what if we need to drive to the hospital, what if the umbilical cord is wrapped around its neck, if I hemorrhage?

There's more pressure now, more pain. I feel faint so I grip the table leg with one arm and slide down the wall and glance at Lenn and he has fear in his eyes now, pure fear.

"Juice!" I scream at him. "Juice!"

He runs to the sink and makes strong lime juice and helps me to sip it. I reach down and touch the top of my own baby's head and it is the most perfect thing I have ever touched in my life. A smooth, dry head; perfectly formed. I've touched my child and that makes all the difference somehow and the agony is still there but it's worth something now.

"What do I do?" he asks.

"Nothing," I say.

"What?"

"Nothing!" I scream at him, saliva spraying toward his armchair, sweat flying from my hair as I whip my head around to face him.

I push hard, there is momentum, the energy in this fenland farm is concentrated on my lower abdomen. There is no power anywhere else to match it, the force of this baby making its way out into the world, opening me, moving lower.

My screams are distant from myself. Not sure if it's the pills or what. I hear them before I make them, screams to topple mountains. I yell and retch and push and grit my teeth and bite down into his rancid leather belt.

"His head's out," says Lenn.

I reach down and touch my baby's face, its nose, its forehead. My mouth breaks into a smile. The pads of my fingertips probe the softness under the baby's chin. I pause, looking down, I can see black hair, fine, wet, matted, bloody.

One more push, two more. Again. My eyelids are scrunched shut. I screech and his belt falls from my mouth and my baby slips out of me and I see a deer in a forest in my mind as I bend forward to touch the little one; a deer mother birthing a fawn in some quiet, protected glen.

I reach to pick up my baby but Lenn takes it and holds it up.

"Ain't breathin'," he says.

I scream and kick out with my good leg, and he hands the baby to me like it's some skinned hare and I take its warm body and turn it around. Turn her around.

"Lass," he says.

I take my finger and scoop fluid from her perfect mouth, from her red lips, and turn her around again, some ancient impulse which I do not question, and I smack her behind and rub her back and she stiffens and wails and I pull her into me and smile the broadest smile anyone has ever seen and we lie there together, just her and me, together.

"It's a lass," he says.

I nod and stroke her tiny head and touch her earlobe, a pearl, and latch her to my breast. She doesn't take right away so I adjust her and hold her and she searches me with her bloodred lips and she finds me.

"I'll get a blanket for her."

He goes upstairs and we are alone. Do not come back, Lenn. Leave us be.

She is drinking from me. I have never done this before but it feels like I have, she is drinking and suckling from me and together we are warm.

He comes back downstairs.

"More stuff comin' out now," he says.

I look down at the eyelids and the nose of my daughter. Eyelids like petals. A nose as perfect as a stone worn smooth by a river. She is the smallest and strongest-looking person I have ever seen and in the moment I hold her on this green tarp I pledge to her my body in its entirety. My soul, as well. Forever. I pledge, unthinking and unsaid, that I will be her mother and her father, her siblings and grandparents and neighbors. I will be her teachers and her priest, and I will not allow harm to visit her. I will not permit it.

"Name's Mary," says Lenn.

He is not one of us. He is not alive in our world or any part of it. Your name may be Mary to him but I will think up the right name for you when he is out plowing his flat fields, when I've studied every pore of you and watched you until my eyes dry over.

I drag the blanket up my midriff and cover her back.

We are as one.

11

She's asleep.

I'm in the single bed in the small back bedroom, a towel wrapped around my waist, a blanket over her back, double thickness, and she's asleep for the first time in her life. I feel her breath on my skin, each exhalation a gift from her perfect lungs. Her heartbeat is fast. Faster than I expected it to be. She is as small as a bird but as complete as anything I have ever seen or imagined. She is miraculous.

When she wakes I carry her—she weighs less than a kitten—to the closet and bring out a pile of terry-cloth diapers, the same ones I use as sanitary napkins, his mother's old cloths. I should have had them prepared but she came so early. I stack them by the storage heater and place her down within the pillow nest I built on the bed and fold a cloth the way I've done a hundred times over the past seven years, and place it inside my underwear, his mother's underwear. Then I take another and fold it the way I've practiced, and place it around her waist, around my daughter's waist, and she stays asleep and she looks so tiny. So perfect. I cannot stop smiling. My ankle is a dull ache in the middle distance, but my heart is swollen with pride for growing this person and bringing her out into the world all on my own and for feeding her and for her sleeping so peacefully like she's been born into a normal home.

I lie with her and curl my body around hers. She makes noises. Safe noises. Contented noises. My stomach is still huge, like I haven't given birth at all, but it's soft now. My mother tore when she had me, she told me she did, and she tore with my sister, and I always expected the same. But I seem to be okay. Tender and numb, the pills doing what they're designed to do, but I'm okay.

"Finished drillin'," he shouts as he enters the house. "Birds never left me alone for one minute, somethin' wrong with 'em I reckon."

I tighten my curl around her, my back a wall between her and him.

"You makin' me a pie or what?"

I don't say anything, I just watch her sleep, her chest moving up and down, her Cupid's bow lips parted slightly, the air pocket sucked in and out as small as a sparrow's cough. He steps upstairs to our small back bedroom. The treads creak and then they stop creaking. He's behind me, watching. Watching us now, not just me, she is now living under his roof, his things, his rules.

"You makin' a pie?"

I close my eyes and feel her cool feet on my belly and her cheek close to the tip of my nose and I pretend to be fast asleep. He watches us. He stays but he does not attempt to wake us, he just observes. And then he walks back downstairs.

I could lie here with her for a hundred lifetimes. She is nothing of him and everything of goodness and I know this with all my soul and she's only been here half a day. I know it.

She wrinkles her nose and I think she might sneeze, but she sniffs and opens her mouth as if for my breast and then she settles down again and rests. Her eyes move beneath her lids. Dreaming.

I've never seen harmony like this in his house. She is a gift and he is not worthy of even knowing what she looks like.

I left the cord downstairs. He offered me a freezer clip and then a pair of scissors that he sterilized in a pan of water on the Rayburn hot plate. We weren't sure if that was necessary but it seemed sensible. I've covered her belly button with veterinary gauze and secured it with masking tape. It's the best I could do.

I have never been so tired or so relieved. A month early, maybe more, but she seems to be perfect. Well, she looks perfect, and she feeds and she sleeps. All the fingers and toes. Some hair on her head, some on her shoulders. A birthmark on the back of her neck. Eyelashes, my sister's eyelashes, and the most exquisite nostrils I have ever seen.

I want to study her like a postgraduate student might study a narrow niche of a subject. Deep and singular. The kind of focus that's difficult to comprehend. I want to know her.

It was three pills in the end, three whole horse pills counting the one I had that morning. I'm as strong as a bloody elephant, so it turns out. I have the anatomy of some long-forgotten mammoth, some killer whale of the cold, arctic deep, I am as formidable as a river in full flood. Maybe he sees that now. But I need to be careful. I look at her and I think clearly and that needs to be the way it is from now on, for her sake and for mine. I need to be watchful and alert. Half a pill for the next few days, then a third. Maybe down to a quarter in time but probably a third.

The tarp's still down there unless he's tidied it away. He'll leave it to me, I expect. Blood and other things, a discarded umbilical cord lying like a dead copper snake, sweat, lime juice, placenta, dead leaves.

"Sandwich?" I hear from down the stairs. "Cheese and ham?"

He's offering me a sandwich.

Offering me.

It's not my stomach's spontaneous grumble that surprises me, it's this role reversal, this change. The awful night of my ankle six years ago he wanted sausage and mashed potatoes and he waited until I tried to make it, until I passed out again from the pain in front of his Rayburn.

I uncurl myself from her and sit up on the end of the bed.

"Yes, please."

"Coming up."

I hear the metal clank as he opens the bread bin. I hear the cellophane wrapping come off the thick-cut Mighty White. It rustles. I hear him open the fridge and pull out the presliced cheese and the presliced ham and the margarine. He doesn't ever do these things and I'm sitting on the single bed in the small back bedroom next to my sleeping daughter listening to him make me dinner.

He walks upstairs with two plates and gives one to me, all the time watching her.

He stands in the doorway, resting his immense shoulder against the frame, and we both look at her and we both chew and swallow and it is very quiet in the house. The June light is warm in the window and it casts a glow on one side of her face and the shadow cast by her is small.

"Young'un alright, is she?" he whispers.

"Yes."

"I'll go downtown tomorrow, get the weekly shoppin' done early, we're gettin' low on juice."

I just smile at my baby. I need the bathroom and I want to take her with me, to never have her more than an arm's length from me. But she's fast asleep and I think she needs the rest.

"Can you watch her for me," I say. "I need the bathroom."

"Of course I can."

I hobble to the door and he stands aside and I hop to the banister and pull myself down, looking back at each step, seeing her there, alone, unprotected, fragile. My right foot's in bad shape. Worse than usual. If I put any weight on it then it feels like it'll snap right off. I grip the wall to get to the toilet and then I sit down, one foot facing forward, the other to the bath, my toes blue, the blood supply worse with each year that passes.

I'm leaking fluids. Not as much as I expected, but still. I clean myself up and splash cold water on my face and my neck and a force pulls me up toward the stairs. It's been long enough, too long. I need to see her breaths, her chest moving, her eyelids, her nostrils. I need to give her my warmth.

He's still in the doorway watching her. I hobble up and pass him and she's still asleep, still shielded by a ring of pillows.

I check her breathing and it is shallow and fast but she seems well. I would give a kidney and a lung for her to be checked by a doctor right now, a full checkup, some kind of report or certificate telling me she's healthy, that she's not in any pain, that she'll live, thrive, and that she'll never be anything like him.

He finishes his sandwich and I finish mine. I'm tired. She'll be awake soon for a feed and I need rest, I need to recharge.

"I need to sleep now," I say.

"Get another blanket. Clear night, colder than it looks out there." He points to the window.

I go to the storage closet. On the right side are his mother's things, on the left side are my stack of letters from Kim-Ly, bound with baling twine, and my battered copy of *Of Mice and Men*. I take a blanket from his mother's side and hold the doorframe and turn around and he is holding my child.

"What," I breathe, a broken whisper. "What are you doing?"

"Holding me daughter," he says, looking down at her with a

smile, her whole body supported by his two big hands, his gnarled cuticles curled up around her head and her thighs.

I step to him. "Let me take her, she needs a feed."

"She's a strong young'un," he says, lifting his chin to look at me. "And if you ever try to leave this cottage with her"—he moves one of his hands so his flat fingers curl around my baby's neck, the rough tips meeting over her tiny throat—"I'll sink her in the dike."

I rush to him and take her and he releases her with no struggle and I turn my back on him and pull her tight into my chest, into my belly.

"You understand?"

I nod, my back to him.

"I said, do you understand?"

"Yes," I say.

"Right then," he says. "Now that's out the way, I can tell you somethin' I been meanin' to get out for a while now."

I turn my head, my back still to him, my spine a guardrail, my daughter starting to nuzzle for my breast in her sleep.

"You seem quite pleased with yourself, Jane. Quite happy with all this."

I frown at him.

"And now I know you ain't leavin', you'll never leave now, not after what I just said to you."

She finds my nipple and latches on and starts to suckle.

"It's your sister, you see," he says. "Well, she ain't in Manchester." What?

"She got sent back didn't she, got herself deported about five year ago, she's not here in England no more."

"What?" I say, turning to face him, my shawl falling open. "You're lying."

"She's gone back where you both come from, back to the jungle, not here, just you and me here, and now little Mary and all."

"No," I say. "I have her letters."

"All old, they are," he says. "I've been rationin' them out cuz there's no dates on them. I burned the ones with news, stuff that would give the game away, burned a page here and a whole letter there. She wrote you a lot, daft woman. Kept you goin' all these years though, I'll give her that." He looks at my baby. "But now I've run out. I had a couple letters left but I just burned them now on the Rayburn. She ain't livin' in England no more, Jane. Got deported years back. Sent home to where you both come from. Sent back. Not legal, see. You ain't got nobody here no more except for me and the young'un. You just got us two and you ain't leavin' unless you want young Mary sunk in the bottom of that dike."

I t is the dead of night and the light from the window of the small back bedroom is dim and quiet.

Lenn's snoring in the other room.

I asked for half a pill before he went to bed and he gave it to me and now I'm propped up against the wall on this single bed, feeding, thinking, hurting. Numb but not numb enough.

My sister was sent back years ago? How? My reality was a lie, my aspirations, projected onto her, lived through her slow journey toward freedom, was a trick of the light. She didn't even get close to being free of her debt. Now she'll be burdened with it for life. The debt with none of the opportunities. I asked him how she was deported, on an airplane or via some more dangerous method. Officially or unofficially. He didn't know. I pray she was put on a plane with her things and sent home to Vietnam. But in my head she was put inside a shipping container like the one we arrived inside. Shipped by greedy men from harbor to harbor, sick, freezing cold, told to keep silent, threatened with no water and no food.

My baby's feeding well. Her strength is growing. I can feel the power in her lips, the vigor of her tiny mouth as she suckles from me. I enjoyed one day of happiness with her. Lenn gave me that one day. I have lost a sister and gained a daughter. He had a hand in both.

She unlatches and is asleep at my breast. Her mouth is open and her cheeks are hot and red and full, her body warm against mine, her fine hairs sweaty in the crook of my arm. She smells of milk. Sweetness. I can hear her tiny vole breaths and his grumbling snores and nothing else.

I sleep when she sleeps and the pills help with the layers of pain inside my body and my head and my stomach. I am broken inside and out. My poor sister.

My baby's diaper changes are a practical trial I didn't expect. The feedings go well and the sleeping seems to be fine, and she hardly screams or cries, like she already understands that he won't like it and she's trying to make my life as easy as possible as I digest the abject horror of what he's told me. Each diaper is stained black. The black tar on her backside is so thick and sticky I can hardly remove it. When I rub I leave red marks and I worry she'll cry out but she doesn't. I wipe her with paper and water, and when that doesn't work I try with a flannel, one of Lenn's. That works a little but it leaves her raw. Is this black liquid normal? I want a wise old nurse to tell me this is normal and the baby will be fine and that she will grow to be a happy woman someday, a woman with her own life.

The next day he goes out early to start the barley harvest. This month has been hot and the yield looks decent, so he says. I sit on the single bed reading *Of Mice and Men* to her at a whisper. The part where George and Lennie tell Candy all about the rabbits. About the plans. The dream. She feeds and makes contented noises and I read on. Kim-Ly has been sent home and I feel like Lenn did it even though he's just the one telling me about it. He withheld the news.

He used my hope for my sister against me. Kim-Ly was deported and now I'm George at the end of the book when he shoots Lennie and is left alone with his alfalfa hopes and I always thought I would be Lennie and she would be George. I will read this book to my daughter over and over again. I will not let him take it from me. She needs it. I'll teach her about life from this one book if I have to. I will reread it so I know it by heart and so will she.

"I'll have me sandwich early," he shouts up the stairs. "Make it a double."

I bring her down with me, patting her narrow back, urging her to burp, a towel draped over my right shoulder. I've mastered this now. I inch down the stairs on my behind like a child, gripping her, ignoring the banister. It's tough on my ankle but I won't fall this way, I won't crush her.

"I'll take Mary," he says.

"No," I say. "She's hungry. I'll feed her and make your lunch."

He looks like he might say something but then swallows his words. I carry her with her face to my breast inside my shirt but she's not feeding, just nuzzling.

I give him the plate of sandwiches and a bag of salted chips.

"How did she get sent back?" I ask.

He chews with his mouth open and frowns at me.

"My sister."

"How do I know?" he says. "Weren't legal. This ain't her country so they sent her packin'. Happens all the time down at Frank Trussock's farm."

He looks at my baby, her face turned toward my skin, away from his gaze.

"When you bathin' again?"

I close my shirt and turn from him. What is this man? This beast?

"Not for a while," I say. "It's like a wound. Has to heal."

He says nothing and eats and then leaves his plate on the table and the empty bag on the plate and walks out.

I stand at the front door with the sun on my face.

"You'll walk up that track one day, little one," I say to her. "You'll walk off into the rest of your life, away from all this. And I'll be at your side. Until that day we'll be here together and I'll be yours, all yours."

There's a truck in the distance driving from right to left and the crops between me and it are lime green and full-grown and they've thickened up so much I can't see any brown. I step out and look around. A warm breeze. The land, everything from my broken foot up to the horizon, is his. He shapes what I get to live in. I walk a few steps outside and lean against the shed and cover her head with my palm to shade her from the sun. The skies are all mine. He has no say in the skies, no drilling or harvesting. No input whatsoever. The land is his and the skies are mine, hers and mine. The horizon, the fine strip where the two meet, that's everything else.

I lay her on the plastic-wrapped sofa and surround her with cushions while I wash the cloths. She's using eight a day and I'm using three, so I have to keep on top of it. The hit from the horse pill is in full flow and it's like the pain from my crushed ankle is now in another room, the half-cellar maybe, under me, still close by but there's something in between it and us. I hang the wet cloths on the line with his mother's wooden clothespins, and check on her, and soon I'll need to give her a real name. The marrow inside my bones is straining to call her Kim-Ly. But this is a selfish thought. A bad thought. I've lost my sister now, I admit that, and it'd be cheap comfort to name my baby after her. I must resist the urge. It's like when you lose a precious pet and then you yearn to buy an infant version to replace it immediately, to give it the same name, and then you stop yourself. I'll think of some other names tonight during the quiet feeds.

I haven't picked up the letters yet because they will break me. I want to read them forensically, to piece together how I mistook two years of her writing for seven.

My baby cries out for me and I sit with her on the sofa and feed her. She's ravenous hungry, her lips finding me immediately. It's like she's pushing my body, driving it to produce more milk for her, and when I look at her I see Kim-Ly. It's only natural. I cared for Kim-Ly like a second mother when I was a child, helping Mom, keen to step up. But here in this forgotten windswept place my baby only has me.

I'm not cutting back on the pills. I know I said I would, for the sake of the baby, but I can't collapse now. I can't crumble. So I'll stick to three-quarters for the time being. I'll be okay.

"Best get the washin' in," he says, walking through into the main room carrying shopping bags from the Spar shop in the next village. "Mizzlin' and spittin' out there."

I walk to the door.

"Leave Mary with me," he says, taking her from me. "That's it, Mary, come to your father."

You are not her father. You are nothing. I am her family.

I turn and hobble as quickly as I can out the door and pull the damp cloths off the line, letting the wooden clothespins fly off in all directions. I walk back inside, my right ankle dragging in the dirt, and throw the cloths, his mother's cloths, down on the table, and take her from him and whisper to her in Vietnamese that it's all okay now.

"None of that," he says. "This is England and she'll speak proper English like me and the rest of us. I'll have none of that other stuff, none of them foreign words, you'll mess with her head."

I nod but my eyes are steel and my focus bores into his forehead and out through the other side. I will speak to my child how I see fit and you will have no say in it.

"Get the fish on, then," he says.

I stoke the Rayburn and push in willow sticks and put away the food shopping. I pleaded with him to buy some things for the baby but he has not bought them. He buys things he thinks we need: sliced ham and toilet paper and chips and rich tea biscuits. But he won't buy disposable diapers or wet wipes or diaper rash creams. He says the Spar shop doesn't stock those things. He says we don't need them.

When the fire's hot enough I cook his boil-in-the-bag cod in parsley sauce. We eat it at the table once he's reviewed the tapes. We eat in silence with frozen Birds Eye peas and boiled potatoes. I'm ravenous. Last night I ate half a pack of rich tea biscuits and a whole jug of water when I was feeding my child. The hunger was immense. There is a heat radiating from me and from her, an energy, a force, a cycle of milk and food, and I need to keep feeding the fire.

He's bought Arctic roll for dessert. It's some kind of sweet cake wrapped around a column of ice cream. He buys it sometimes. He likes it. We eat and my back tooth starts to hurt like someone's stabbing it with a needle.

The baby's backside is red. I bathe her in the tub, my hand under her whole body. I want to make use of the hot water because we let the Rayburn die down after dinner these hot days, otherwise we can't sleep. I check the water because it comes out of the faucet scalding hot, and then I give my first child her first bath. She screams and I smile and soothe her. Then I wrap her in a towel and take her upstairs, one slow step at a time, my hand gripping the banister to save both our lives, and get her to the small back bedroom. I blow on her skin and fold a fresh cloth to form a diaper and wrap her and use a safety pin, one of his mother's, to keep it secure.

She's warm and calm.

I hear him unlock the TV cabinet downstairs and then lock away the key in the key box bolted to the wall by the front door.

"TV's on," he says.

I sit with my baby and almost fall asleep holding her. This is a whole new level of weary. I start to feed her and he says, "I said, TV's on, come downstairs, come on."

"We're going to sleep," I call down.

"The heck you are. Come downstairs, a bit of television will do you some good."

I wriggle to the end of the bed and look at my foot. The fluid around the joint is cold to the touch. The bones are snapped and the muscles are torn and the foot may as well be someone else's. If I get out of here I expect some kind doctor will amputate it and that will be the best thing all around.

"Jane."

My name isn't Jane.

"I'm coming."

I shuffle downstairs holding her tight to me.

"Sit down right here." He pats the side of the armchair.

"Lenn, I can't, not with her. I'll sit on the sofa."

"Best part of the day, a bit of TV and all of us together. You'll sit down here where I tell you to."

I get to his chair and try to lower myself but my legs are too weak and I collapse and fall awkwardly on my right foot and I wail with the pain and then the baby starts crying, her tears wet against my chest.

"Mary's hungry," he says.

I bite down on the inside of my cheeks until I taste blood. I latch her on and she feeds and makes cooing noises and my foot feels like I've broken some malformed bone, some fusion of tissue, some approximation of an ankle joint. He pats my head and I can feel his eyes on my breast, his eyes above my head looking down at me feeding my child as I sit on his bare floorboards.

"It's nice, ain't it, the three of us sittin' here for an evenin'? Not a bad life, is it?" He pats my head again, stroking my unwashed hair. "We'll see the rest of this game, then I'll be off to feed the pigs."

I watch the screen with tears in my eyes. An empty feeling inside me. Tiredness. From the routines but also from the hopelessness. She sucks and I unclench my teeth and taste the blood on my tongue and feel the back tooth loose in its socket and I think about killing him. Before, when he threatened that my sister would get sent home, he'd said that his friend Frank Trussock would know something's wrong because they speak every day so if Lenn didn't check in then Kim-Ly would get reported. But now Lenn can't use that against me so he's threatened my child instead. That means I can't try to escape, the stakes are too high. I can't make it out of here. Before my baby I always had the option to kill myself, maybe in the dike, but then he'd have sent my sister back. Now I can't kill myself because my daughter would have to endure an unimaginably cruel life and she'd have to endure it alone. But I could end him. The risk is that we'd be stuck here with nothing, that the supplies would dry up and the food would run out and I'd have to wait for some chance visitor. Or his friend Frank Trussock. Maybe I'd have to fight Frank. Protect us both. Lenn pats my head again and makes comments about one of the snooker players and I sit feeding my daughter and planning his death.

13

My daughter is growing stronger and she needs a name. She deserves one.

I try to picture my childhood. The colors, and the shape of the roof on our house and the scent of lotus flowers in the summertime and the way my father would chase us around the garden, hiding behind bamboo clusters and pretending he couldn't find us and then sprinting out and roaring and laughing and running away again like any other neighborhood boy. My daughter's name will come to me.

We had lean years when I was young. After my brother was born, we had little money for shoes or new clothes. But we never went hungry. Later on my father told me how he was often anxious for the family. But I never noticed. My parents either shielded us from their worries or else their partnership was so strong that they leaned on each other. A couple who found one another after a party at a riverside restaurant in 1989.

He's left a pill out for me by the kitchen sink. I take it and go upstairs with her for a midday nap. Her eyes are everywhere. I shift up the stairs one at a time, hot pain in my foot, hot pain in my mouth, and she's looking up at me, directly into my eyes, at my face, taking me in.

We lie down together and I feed her. The pill's working. It's a big dusty square pill now, the supplier's changed. Lenn assures me it's the same medicine inside but I think these ones are stronger.

When I wake up my mouth is dry. My lips are stuck together and they're attached to the pillow of the single bed in the small back bedroom. It takes me a moment to remember where I am. Who I am. I'm in that fuzzy state you feel when you're almost asleep, perhaps you're entering sleep, and then a noise wakes you and you're awash with vagueness and warmth and you long to preserve that quiet buzz.

Where's my baby?

I turn and feel her beneath my chest, under me. My weight is bearing down on her. I prop up on one elbow, panic in my chest. What have I done? I scoop her out and she's still.

Quiet.

No.

What have I done?

Her eyes are closed. I bring her to my lips, her mouth to mine to feel her breath but there is no breath. She's warm, but it's my warmth.

"No, no," I say but the words fall flat from my mouth.

The room spins.

I hold her in front of my eyes and squeeze her and then her tiny nose wrinkles and she snorts and her mouth parts.

I lift her eyelid. She snaps it back shut. I take her to my breast and she opens her mouth and suckles but she doesn't really drink. She is alive. Waves of relief; each one stronger than the one before. But I am suddenly sober and clearheaded and my God, Thanh Dao, you almost killed your own daughter.

My blood is solid in my veins with what could have been. These new pills. What's in them? He's never even told me what species of beast they were manufactured for. The lack of information makes me livid. A man controlling me in a dozen different ways. Ten dozen.

I have to wean myself off the drugs or I'll accidentally kill my own child. My sleep is too deep, too unreal.

She disconnects from my breast and there's a drip of milk hanging from her lip and another on her chin.

"I'm sorry," I whisper to her. "I'm so, so sorry. I'll do better."

She opens her eyes and looks at me as if to say you are already perfect and I am the safest and luckiest child that has ever lived.

"Get yourself down here."

I wipe my eyes and check her again and she's fine so we get down the stairs together on my backside.

"Tapes say you done nothin' this whole afternoon."

"I'm not well," I say. "My leg. I was resting with Mary upstairs, Lenn. I had to."

"You got all night to rest together in that back room. Day's for workin'." He points to the Rayburn stove. "And you let that go out, didn't you? Don't care about me dinner, not bothered I've been toilin' out there in the fields on a day like this with that weather comin' down off the salt marshes, not bothered, are you? Well, if I don't eat then none of us eat, don't forget that."

I look at the clock and it says ten past five.

"I'm sorry, Lenn."

"Get the dinner on, I'm famished."

I take a long match from the half-empty box of Swan Vestas and light the Rayburn. My baby's asleep on the plastic-wrapped sofa, cushions all around. I fry his ham and his eggs in his mother's old cast-iron skillet and I roast his frozen fries in the top oven even though the fire's not burning hot enough to do a proper job of it.

He's upstairs banging around. I will the stove hotter, but it's coming from too cold a starting place and his eggs aren't the way he likes them and the clock's ticking on the wall and she'll need her next feed soon.

He comes downstairs.

"Ain't hot enough, is it?"

"It's getting there," I say. "I've put more wood on."

He takes *Of Mice and Men* out from his back pocket.

"Reckon this'll help it along."

Tears form in the corners of my eyes, tears I wouldn't have known a month ago, but they come easier now for some reason, they're closer to the surface either because of her or because of what happened to my sister or probably both.

"Please don't," I say.

"Book or sister's letters, one or the other, you can pick, up to you. If you'd done your chores we would have nothin' to talk of, ain't my doin'."

I point to the sofa. To the perfect, cooing baby framed by thread-bare cushions.

"I want her to read it one day."

He smiles.

"She'll be too busy for your book readin', she'll be workin' for a livin' like her father has to. She won't be idle, I'll be makin' sure of that, you mark my words. Now, open the hatch."

I open the fire door of the Rayburn. At this point years ago I still had hope that he'd relent, find some mercy. I remember when he burned the photo of my family, seventeen members all together—cousins and uncles and grandparents—when he burned it for me trying to break into the phone he boxed inside a metal case and bolted to the floor joists. I went at it ferociously with tools from his shed and I didn't even get close to being able to pull out the receiver.

He steps to the stove and looks at the book and turns it over and looks at the back cover, at the curled edges, the typeface, the photo of Steinbeck, and then he looks at me and tosses it into the fire. The flames flare and I watch the book blacken, each page crisping and shrinking and turning amber and gray all at once.

His fries are too pale.

"What's up with this, then?" he says, pointing at his plate. "What do you call this?"

I say nothing. I eat my fries, my eggs, my ham. I need it, I need it for her. I glance at him and he's looking at my right hand. I look down and I'm gripping my dinner knife so tight my knuckles are white and the knife's trembling on the table. He stands up.

"Same thing as before, you know that, don't you? Anything happens to me, say a nasty accident or somethin' when I'm fast asleep, and I don't check in with old Frank Trussock, he'll do to Mary what I talked about, he'll make sure of it." He looks over at the sofa. "We're a happy family here, Jane, so don't go havin' no daft ideas, do you understand me?"

I nod.

"Right, make sure you do. And another thing, it's about time you had a good hot bath. Get one run now that the stove's goin' and get yourself clean, woman. I'll take care of the young'un. Go on."

I'm still holding the knife. I don't move, don't say anything.

"You want them letters burnin' and all, do you, cuz that's how it's goin'."

I stand up and clear the plates and run a bath. I need her letters. I came here with seventeen possessions and I have one left. One possession and one daughter and that's what I'll be leaving with one day once I figure out how. And if Frank ever turns up here I'll kill him and I'll kill Lenn right where they stand. I'll bury them both out by the ash pile and I'll not think twice about it.

I lie in the bath and my ribs shimmer beneath the surface. The hot water, heated by my only book, my precious incinerated book, helps with my ankle; it helps maybe twenty percent. I lie here with the door wide open, a draft around my neck, but I'm warm and I feel like I might sleep. My eyelids are heavy. She's in the main room with him but there's nothing I can do about that, nothing at all. I wash myself. Rain beats down on the corrugated-iron roof above and I top up the hot water, steaming as it comes out of the faucet.

My tongue can move my back tooth. It hurts but the sister tooth on my left side hurts a hundred times more. I need a pediatric nurse to look over my daughter, and I need an orthopedic surgeon and a dentist for myself.

I step out of the bath and dry myself on his mother's old gray towel and the floor feels soft and lumpy underfoot. Something's rotten down there. Something bad. Covered over. I pull on my nightie, his mother's, and wrap my hair in a towel. The beat of the rain on the roof intensifies to a dull roar and the temperature drops in the walls.

He's holding her.

He's sitting in his armchair with her in his arms and she seems fine with it. He's smiling down at her but his massive body is motionless. Perfectly still. An innocent child and a monstrous statue gripped in an absurd staring contest.

"Let's get up them stairs then," he says. "You want me to carry Mary up or do you want to do it?"

"I'll take her."

He hands her over to me, the muscles in his forearms bulging against her head. I hobble upstairs and he comes up a few minutes later.

"Feed her up good and then you sleep back in your own bed tonight."

I don't look at him.

She's hungry and I move her to my breast, a pillow propped underneath her to save my back and my arm. I feed her and she falls asleep and her mouth gapes open very slowly and she lies there next to my skin with her bright red cheeks, her heat, her plumpness, and I gaze at her every eyelash.

I put her down. Four pillows encircle her, another on the floor just in case, and then I close my nightie and walk over to the landing.

He's standing at the window looking out toward the locked halfway gate and the road beyond. The thin cotton sheet is folded on the bed and his towel is next to it.

"Lenn, I'm not ready yet, I'm—"

"You're alright. I'll be soft with you, come on."

His voice is gentle. He doesn't want to wake the baby.

I'm still not used to this and I never will be. Each incidence is a life-changing act. I'm strong for my daughter but I will have vengeance on this man. I will make him pay.

I pull my nightie up over my head and slide under the sheet, my eyes prickling, the distance too great between me and Huong. My daughter. Huong. That's my daughter's name. It just came to me. I smile a shallow smile. Huong Dao. She is asleep in the next room and I'm her mother and I'm stuck in here.

I drag the sheet up my body so only my top half is covered.

I will protect Huong and I will help her.

I sense him move closer and I turn my face to the wall like I always do, and I can feel his breath on my thigh. I try to imagine myself away. I try with the epidural but it fails because I need to listen out for little Huong, I need to be completely present for my daughter.

She is quiet.

Huong makes a noise and I lift my head. She starts crying. Wailing. His hands are on my hips now.

"Ignore it," he says, the words breathed onto me.

I bite my lip and listen to her and I can feel her wanting me. This is excruciating. I can't be here, ignoring her. She wants me. My body is tearing itself apart to be with her. Huong's two weeks old, she needs me.

He brings his hands around and under me.

My tears come. I want to clamp my legs together so hard I squeeze the last sour breath out of him. Snap him in two. Destroy him. Huong wails now, even louder than before, and I feel it in my chest. I'm leaking, warm milk pouring into the sheet making it translucent, running down my sides, down my stomach. She needs me.

He backs away.

"What the . . ."

I turn my head and look at him through the sheet, his outline. What more does he want from me? Huong's screeching, coughing.

"You're leakin' somethin' out of you," he says.

"I know."

"Don't know what that is," he says pulling the sheet down over my lower half, stepping away from me, "but it ain't normal. You got some kind of wound or somethin', you're leakin' all over, you need to wash yourself."

I wrap the sheet around me and stand up.

"Sort yourself out, woman," he says. "Keep yourself clean." He pulls on his jeans and his shirt and sets off down the stairs. "I'm off to feed the pigs and then I'll be back. Make sure you're in that back bedroom."

I stagger to her as fast as I can and hold her and bring her to me and sit back against the wall and she sobs and finds me and latches on and we sit there listening to his quad race off toward the distant pig barn.

14

Huong is growing stronger.

I have a craving to know what she weighs, how long she is. That's normal in Vietnam, you get to know these things on the day of the birth. Data. Hard statistics. Officially recorded in the system. Things I can hang on to. Numbers to remember and share with curious grandmothers and uncles who in turn compare them to other family members. But I have no idea. She seems healthy enough, although I do worry that her thirst is too intense. I worry that she's dependent on the horse pills and that she needs my milk to get her dose like I need my three-quarters of a pill each day just to be able to function.

It's midafternoon and the sun is beaming through the front window. He hasn't asked me to stay in his front bedroom since that night. I feel more vulnerable than ever with my ankle pain and my toothache and my possessions now burned down to one. The letters. If I lose them I'll lose the last contact I may ever have with Kim-Ly and I will lose the last possession, the last piece of myself that exists in this damp featureless world.

I mop the floor and glance at her. Huong's awake, snuffling on the sofa, her hands opening and closing. I slop the mop in the bucket of soapy water and wipe the floors clean and she's listening to the noise the water makes on the floorboards. The squeak and also the drips as they find their way between the boards and into the dark half-cellar below. She can grip my finger now. She's strong, I think, a concentrated bundle of power and potential. I just have to help her reach it.

The sunlight disappears and the room darkens. He's there at the front window. Then the light floods back in and the front door opens.

"I'll be done balin' in about an hour and a bit, then I'll come in. I'll fix your mouth tonight, I said I would and I will."

"Let's wait one more day," I say.

"Your rotten teeth ain't doin' that young'un no good. I'll whip them out before they get you both sick. I did it for me mother and she were fine, didn't make a squeak. I'll have them out after me tea."

Maybe it's for the best. I think they're wisdom teeth, bottom row, right at the back, one on each side. Last time I saw a dentist was with my mother and my brother nine years ago. The dentist also taught at the local medical university. She was kind, strict but kind, and she had a way of making me relax. I've only ever had fillings and routine checkups. Never an extraction.

I let the floors dry. My fear is that I'll put too much weight on my bad foot one of these days and it'll snap even more. Or twist farther around. I pad flat-footed to Huong and pick her up and inch up the stairs. To my letters. I sit on the bed with my back to the cool wall and pull a letter from under the pillow. I unfold it and stuff the pillow under my arm and let her latch on. I need to memorize her words like I did with *Of Mice and Men*. I need to read them and read them so I can recite them to Huong when she's older. I have a responsibility to her, so she knows her aunt, so she understands some of our heritage, so she knows the country beyond these endless flatlands, so she learns good English.

My mouth hurts and my foot aches but I am content. The warmth of her on my body, the two of us reconnected, the smell of her scalp, the sound of her sucking, the beat of her tiny pigeon heart against mine. And the words. Kim-Ly was a good writer. This letter tells of the city park she drives through on the way from the nail salon to the apartment. She has to pay for the transit each week, it's deducted automatically from her wages just like accommodation and heating. It's not optional. She tells me about the colors of the trees and the wet grayness of the walls and the memorial statues. She writes of the squealing children on the roundabout and the kind old man who feeds the pigeons every single day. Perhaps I should have suspected that these were two years' worth of letters instead of five but I never did. Perhaps I should have seen the truth in the seasons, in the slow progress. But, as in this letter, much of what she writes is reminiscence because I think she wanted to comfort me. She wrote about Dad's jokes and Mom lecturing us about homework and the way my brother used to ride his bike straight through the house as a young boy.

I slide my finger into Huong's tiny palm and she grips it.

"Don't ever let go," I whisper to her.

I take her downstairs and let her sleep on the sofa. It'll just be twenty or thirty minutes but it's enough time for me to prepare dinner.

I peel potatoes at the sink. My eyes are heavy and it's getting misty out there in the end fields, the ones out toward the pig barn. The mists are straight lines, razor thin. They hang over the fields and block the long-distance view. They connect the land to the sky and I can feel autumn in the air.

The Rayburn's glowing. I throw in another batch of willow and close the vents to settle it down. The chicken's in and the potatoes are in. The water's boiling on the top ready for the peas and the gravy's good and hot.

Pain flares in my jawbone. It's not like my ankle pain, this is someone pushing a dirty blade straight into my flesh and probing a nerve. The sharpness jolts into my head. I hold my chin in my hands and dig my fingernails into my temples and then Huong starts to cry.

Her diaper's full.

I take her to the floor and pull out a fresh cloth from the stash I keep underneath the plastic-wrapped sofa along with a bowl of water and a roll of paper towels. I unpin the cloth. I am very, very tired. It's not black tar anymore, it's green. Her rashes are horrendous. Weeping sores. I mop her up and dab the skin but she is red raw and I blow on her wounds, on her bumps and lesions, but she is screaming so hard her tongue is sticking out of her mouth like a stiff beak.

I squint with pain as my own teeth burn, the nerves exposed.

I blow on Huong's skin and tell her she'll be okay and she'll be better now, but when I pick her up there's blood on the new diaper. Blood from the rash.

"I've had it for today," says Lenn, hanging up his jacket, pulling off his boots. "Combine will need some oil before tomorrow."

"She needs cream," I say.

"Cream? What?"

"Mary. She needs cream for her diaper rash, she's bleeding."

"Don't be daft. Best have it natural, that's what me mother always did, none of them fancy potions and lotions. You keepin' her clean enough, are you?"

"She needs cream," I say, my jaw set. "From the Spar shop in the village. Please, Lenn. I'll do anything you ask, just buy her some baby cream." I soften my voice. "Please, Lenn."

He looks at me and then over at the Rayburn.

"That bird cooked?"

"Ten minutes," I say.

We eat, her feeding from me at the table. He watches. He doesn't try to hide his gaze. I force myself to swallow peas and gravy and a little chicken but I can't really chew, just bite with my front teeth. I know I need food for her, for my milk, for her bones to grow and for her mind to develop so I eat what I can.

"Wasn't bad," he says. "Now then. You get this cleaned up and then I'll fix your teeth."

I'm resigned to this. What else can I do? What options do I have?

She's asleep on the sofa when he brings in the newspapers and spreads them under the pine chair I just sat on to eat my dinner. I try not to think of her rash, her sores, the weeping wounds that show I am failing her.

"Another half pill," he says, placing half a tablet on the table with a glass of water.

I take it.

He removes a pair of pliers from his trouser pocket.

"You need to sterilize them first," I say, my eyes wide open. "They need to be sterile, Lenn."

He takes them to the Rayburn and slides the kettle onto the hot plate and waits for it to boil. He pours water over the serrated ends of his pliers in the sink. They're rusted and the rubber handles are split.

"Open your mouth as wide as it'll go," he says.

I tip my head back and hook my good foot around the chair leg.

"Wider," he says.

I open my mouth to the point where the hinges of my lips hurt. He looks inside my mouth. I want to bite him.

"Back two you reckon?" he says. "Any more, is it?"

I shake my head.

He places his left hand over my face, his fingers pushing down into my eye socket and my cheekbone and my temple.

"Brace yourself then," he says.

I feel the metal of the pliers on my tooth, the loose one, the bleeding one. The pliers feel hot and they feel enormous, like someone rubbing a rough hammer against my molars. He opens his tool and grips my tooth and pushes down harder onto my face with his left hand.

The tooth comes out.

I taste blood in my mouth and swallow and he takes his left hand off my face and my tongue moves back to probe the hole.

"Nothing to it," he says, holding the tooth up for inspection with its absurd depth, its long unhuman roots attached.

"Now, the other one."

I swallow again, my own blood lining my throat. Some of the pain has disappeared.

"Open," he says.

His hand's there on my face again, pushing my head down into my neck. The metallic teeth of the pliers scrape along my own teeth and then they open. Pain surges through me from my tooth, my non-loose tooth. He grips it and pushes down onto my face and pulls.

My God, the pain.

My spine compressed beneath this man's palm.

I weep.

He readjusts his grip on my face and on the pliers and yanks the tooth upward and twists it and my vision turns fuzzy at the edges. I want this to stop.

Huong's crying now. There's more blood in my mouth and he opens the pliers and grabs the tooth and pulls it back and forth and I close my mouth around it because the pain is too much to bear. He retracts the pliers and pries my jaw open.

"Don't mess around, we're almost done here. Swallow this."

Something's on my tongue. I swallow hard and the pill fragment scratches my gullet on the way down. I swallow again and there's more blood in my mouth. Warm, metallic. He grips the tooth and I look into his eyes, his watery blue-gray eyes, and he pulls and keeps pulling and I can hear Huong screaming and then my vision goes dark. He pauses. I hold the chair beneath me and he yanks the tooth again and says something I can't hear. There's a knocking noise. He strains with the pliers. And then everything goes black.

My eyelids open.

I blink and clear my eyes.

I wiggle my jaw and the pain is gone and now my face just aches and my gums are raw. The deep pain, the bone-nerve-jaw pain, is over.

I sit up.

Where is she?

I look around the small back bedroom. How did I get up here? I scoot to the end of the bed and stand up, my balance a little unsteady.

"Lenn," I say, peering into his bedroom. Nothing.

I hold the banister and ease myself down the stairs, my right foot hanging in midair as I hop down.

Huong's crying now, she can sense me. I move into the kitchen and she's lying on the sofa surrounded by cushions, just like before. She screams at me and I can feel warm milk dribbling down my stomach, my shirt wet. I get to her and kiss her forehead and hold her to my chest. She is frantic for milk, screaming, probing with her lips pursed. She latches on and sucks.

But the screaming continues.

"Help me!"

I stand bolt upright with Huong still suckling.

"What?" I say. Is this the pills? "Who said that?"

The front door opens and Lenn walks inside and brings through two bags of Spar shopping and places them down on the pine table. My two teeth are sitting there next to the bags atop a bloodstained tissue.

"Shhh," I say. "Listen."

But the voice is gone.

It could be the drugs but I think I heard something. A voice. A *Help me!*

"What?" he says, rummaging inside the Spar bag. "Sit down," he says.

I sit back down on the sofa and I can hear someone sobbing, someone weeping.

"Ain't doing this regular so don't get yourself used to it, but here."

He sits down hard in his armchair. The sobbing's still there in the background like a TV on in another room. But the TV's in this room and it's locked in the cabinet in the corner. He reaches up and passes me something encased in his rough hand.

A small tub of Vaseline.

"For young'un."

Tears form in my eyes. It is the best thing I have seen in my life.

"Thank you," I say.

I try to detach her from my breast to apply some to her backside but she won't let me. She's famished.

"How long was I asleep for?" I ask.

"Dunno, about twelve hours or somethin', you went right under."

Twelve hours?

"But, Mary?"

He smiles and taps his head. "Bringed her up to you, didn't I? Bringed her up to you and put her on your chest for a drink, every few hours or so, you never woke up, never stirred. She were alright, we made a pretty good team, Mary and me."

I look down. Huong's eyes are closed and her eyelashes are meshed together, the tips almost touching my skin. I can see her pulse in her perfect neck. All that time you were with him? I wasn't awake for you? All that time?

"The pill must have made me black out," I say.

"That and the fact you've got teeth like a horse. Never seen teeth like it, double as long as me mother's, yours was. Almost put me back out gettin' that last one loose, I did."

The sobbing's there again.

From the bathroom? Upstairs?

"Can you hear that, Lenn?"

"You hungry?" he asks.

I nod. I am hungry.

I notice a red scratch on his neck.

"I'll fix you a cheese and ham sandwich and then we'll talk about it."

I finish feeding Huong and lay her down on the sofa and unpin her diaper. It's long overdue. I drag out the paper towels and the bowl of water I keep under the sofa and I clean her and put the dirty paper towel in a Spar plastic bag. The oldest stuff is dried on. I have to moisten it and scrape it off but as gentle as I am with her she screams and yells. Raw skin. Blood.

"I know, little one," I say. "I know. I'm sorry. It's almost over. We have the cream now, you'll be better soon, I promise."

I moisten the paper towel. I can't hear sobbing now, just Huong's screaming. Her face is red. She's crying and the tears are spraying and the ones that settle on her cheeks just sit there and quiver.

My instinct is to smother her backside in Vaseline, to be generous, to bathe her in it. I read the label but it doesn't tell me much. I take my index finger and scoop up some of the thick, smooth gel and apply it to my daughter's wounds. I'm careful. I don't want to rub it in too hard or cause her any more pain, I've done quite enough of that already. I cover the worst of the rash, the dried blood, the blistered flesh, and I wrap her in a new diaper. I hold her and she falls asleep instantly in my arms. Her relief is palpable. I sit with her and the sobbing is still there, close by.

When Huong's deep in sleep, and her eyelids are fluttering, I stand and walk over to the sink and wash my hands.

"Help me, please!" says a voice. "Jane, help me!"

My heart races.

Lenn jumps up from his armchair and runs over to the front door. I watch from the Rayburn as he unbolts the half-cellar door and slams it shut behind him. I listen. No words from him and none from her. Is it Cynth? The red-haired woman with the horse? Must be, no one else knows my name, my false name, the name he imposed upon me.

There's a bang down there. Sniffling.

Then I hear steps up, his boots climbing the steep wooden ladder back up to the half-cellar door, then it opening, then him bolting it shut again.

"Sit down," he says, pointing to the table and the two pine chairs. I sit.

"Mary likes that cream, doesn't she, sleeping alright now with that on her, ain't she?"

"Yes," I say, my eyes darting between his face and the floorboards.

"Who is it?" I whisper.

He shakes his head. "None of your concern, that, Jane. I'll tell you what. Now that you're with young'un I reckon you might need odd extra bits and things, like that cream I got for you at the Spar shop. You keep on doin' your job, lookin' after the house and young Mary, and I'll keep up my end, alright? We'll call it a bargain. About time you had a new thing or two. I'll let you stay in that back bedroom, let you focus yourself on the young'un. And we'll speak no more on it, do you understand?"

There's no noise from the cellar now.

Nothing.

This is where I refuse. Where I stand up and fight. Where I scream to the woman beneath my feet that I will not abandon her, that I will help her.

But, Huong. I have no idea how premature she was when she was born. How vulnerable she still is. If she's to get through these perilous early weeks, if I'm to live, to feed her, nourish her, strengthen her, then I have to be selfish. For her sake. At least until she's a little older. I can't risk her health. I look down at her sleeping face, the roundness of her cheeks, her hair, her soft chin.

"I need a thermometer," I say. "If she gets a fever I need to know how bad it is. I need acetaminophen. It's what my mother used when we had infections. It's important."

He nods.

"I'll see what I can do. You two get up to the back bedroom and I'll make us dinner tonight. Broth and bread. You two get up there for some rest and I'll fix it. No more jabberin'. We're done down here."

We do as he says. We go upstairs and we sleep.

After my blackout and Cynth's screams from the stinking half-cellar, we leave all that behind and rise up and fall asleep. How bad a person am I that I can just sleep after all that? I bend like a waning moon around Huong and she snores her snores and we sleep.

When we go downstairs it's getting dark outside and there's a chill in the floor.

"Broth's good and hot," he says. "Set the table myself, you sit down, take the weight off that foot."

I sit down, Huong is awake and quiet.

We eat the broth, steaming from the heat of the Rayburn, and we mop it up with slices of Mighty White and margarine. When we're done I start feeding Huong and he brings out two tins. I look up at him. What's this?

"Pineapple chunks," he says smiling, placing a teaspoon next to each opened tin. "Good for the young'un, gets vitamins and that from your milk."

I eat. It is fantastic, my first pineapple for years, my first new food type since arriving here on Fen Farm. The juice doesn't sting my gum wounds, they're okay. Healing. My tongue tingles from the acid and it is good.

Is Cynth still down there? Is she alive? There is no noise, no sobbing.

I bathe Huong in shallow tepid water and now that her belly button has healed, the crispy umbilical remnant having fallen away, she looks complete. I dab at her wounds, at her rash. The Vaseline is already helping.

Lenn's moved the dishes to the sink by the time I get back into the main room. It's the first time he's ever done this. I dry Huong and apply a fresh coat of Vaseline, thank God for this cream, this miracle, and put her in a new diaper and dress her in his old baby clothes and lay her on the plastic-wrapped sofa while I wash up.

"I'll put the TV on," he says.

I hear him unlock the key box on the wall of the entrance hall and unlock the TV cabinet and then lock the key back in the key box.

We sit. It's getting damp outside and damp inside so he opens the Rayburn fire door for the first time this season and lets the flames flutter and spit, the light from within licking up the walls and finding the ceiling. We watch the evening news and I sit on the floor with him patting my head and smoothing my hair, my daughter feeding from me, the pineapple still alive on my taste buds.

And then the phone rings.

The box that encases it muffles the noise but I can feel the vibrations through the floorboards.

"Help me!" Cynth screams from under us, her voice more animal than human. "Please!"

The phone rings and rings and we three just sit up here like there's nothing strange happening at all. His hand is still on my head. Rigid. And then the phone stops and she screams something unintelligible.

Lenn stamps the floor with his socked foot so hard it makes me jump. It makes Huong jump a little, too, and then she reconnects and suckles like before.

"This is nice," says Lenn, smoothing my hair. "Not a bad life, is it? We're doing alright."

16

He's almost done with the harvest now. I've been watching from the front door as grains and vegetables are trucked away, him standing at the locked halfway gate in his overalls, positioned between me and the haulage trucks, between us and the haulage truck drivers.

I'm keeping the Rayburn fire going around the clock. Huong gets cold in the night if she drifts from me and, I'm sorry to say, the pills I'm still taking make me sleep so deeply that sometimes I'm not as physically close to her as I'd like to be when I wake up. One-third of a pill was never going to be enough to get me through each day. My nipples are cracked and the left one's bleeding. But it's my ankle. That's why I can't come off the pills. Can't even reduce the dosage. The damp, the October fenland damp creeps into the joints, what's left of them, and makes them swell and stiffen and throb. But it's also her. Downstairs. That ongoing horror. Me not doing anything about it, not being able to think up an ingenious plan to help her, to help Cynth. I end up focusing more on Huong, on her needs from minute to minute so I can avoid thinking what it must be like down there in the stinking half-cellar.

Cynth.

Cynthia.

I must think of her name. If I forget her name then I won't be able to forgive myself. I must offer her that shred of dignity. She still has identity down there in the dark hole beneath this forgotten place. She's still alive. She is not the woman locked in the half-cellar. She is Cynth.

I've never been down there in my seven years on Fen Farm. It's a rule. But I've looked down. When the sun's low by the front door, at the end of a long summer's day, it lights up the hole. I've only peeked down there twice, in the early days, the lucid days, when I had two working ankles, when the bolts were loose, and it was always dark and shockingly cool, and it smelled of spores and decay and wet cardboard and rot.

I'm feeding Huong upstairs and she's starting to bite. She has no teeth but I think I can feel something deep in her gum, some hardening. I pledge to look after her teeth when they come and if ever she needs any professional dental care I will somehow get that for her.

Cynth's down in the half-cellar. If she's sobbing I can't hear it from up here and that's why I'm not in the main room much these days aside from making Lenn his lunch and his tea and keeping the Rayburn fire going. Lenn's eased up on my chores and it's helping my leg a little, even with this damp air.

Cynth is tall.

That's what I keep thinking about: her height. I'm tall myself but she's taller and that half-cellar is as high as an armpit, that's what Lenn told me. You have to bow or crouch or kneel down there, there's nowhere to stand up straight, not even close. She's been there for three weeks and she hasn't once been able to stand erect.

I've used up a whole tub of Vaseline and he's bought me two

more. The diaper rash is all but gone. Huong's more content now but she's feeding like a wild animal might after a drought, sucking and knocking her head against my breast for more milk, to will it out of me. Because it's food? Or because she needs her trace of horse pills just like I do?

I hear the front door creak open.

"Tea," he shouts.

"I'll come down," I say.

"Don't be daft. Do you want some tea, Jane? I'll bring it up to you."

This never happens.

"Thank you."

Huong suckles and I hear him place the kettle on the Rayburn hot plate and I hear Cynth cry out from her darkness. He stamps his foot. Then the noise stops and the kettle starts to whistle and he walks upstairs.

"Young'un drinkin' up good, is she?"

I nod and he places my tea, in the freebie mug from the fertilizer company, down by my bed. His mother's bed.

"Thanks, Lenn."

"Drink it all up, young'un," he says, staring at her. "Big and strong."

"Lenn," I say. "She can't live on scraps. Can I take her down some food?"

"What?"

I nod toward the floor.

His jaw stiffens.

"I'm off down to the shop later, nothin' you fancy? More Vaseline cream for Mary, is it?"

"No, I'm fine."

He walks to the back bedroom storage closet and opens the door and turns to the right, to the slatted wooden shelves holding his mother's things.

"Got clothes here, all me old stuff, moths been at 'em but they'll do. Fix 'em up with some thread maybe. You want me to get you some new wool from the shop?"

I imagine what I can make for Huong. Things with color. Soft, new clothes made by me for her, not by his mother for him. New possessions we can both hang on to. And maybe I can customize the old things, adapt shirts and trousers for when she grows. "Yes, please, Lenn."

He turns around to face me and he has Kim-Ly's letters in his hand. All seventy-two of them. The baling twine holding them hangs down between his fingers like the hair of a doll crushed inside his palms.

"You still want these letters, do you? You're not done with them yet, are you?"

I tense up.

"I want them."

"Well then, don't be pushin' your nose in where it ain't wanted. Nothin' to do with you what's down in the cellar. Keep lookin' after the young'un and keep the house clean and keep makin' me tea, and that's that."

I nod.

"Your last thing, ain't it?"

I nod again. My last possession on this planet.

"Best look after them then, ain't you?"

I look down at Huong. She's still drinking, her cheeks bright red, her hair slick with sweat from the extraordinary heat of us both, from the exertion.

He walks downstairs and drives off in his Land Rover. I lay Huong down surrounded by pillows, a blanket on top, and make my way down each step on my backside. Cynth's quiet underneath the house. I walk to the front door and double-check he's out and then I look at the black iron bolt at the top of the half-cellar door and its twin down near the bottom. There's a noise. Wood creaking. The door moves in its frame.

"Jane? Jane, is that you? Jane? Help me, is that you?"

I open my mouth as if to speak and then look to my right at the camera in the corner of the main room above the locked-away TV. Its red light blinks at me. I close my mouth and lick my lips and squint my eyes and walk back to the kitchen. She says nothing after that. I wash up and dry the pots and feed the fire and rub breast milk into my nipples to try to alleviate the soreness. I would try the Vaseline but I have to keep it for Huong. Years ago, after my ankle but before he burned my sneakers, I asked him for a new bra and he told me his mother's would do me, and I asked again recently, partly because of my back, for one that would fit me, and he said his mother's would still do me, it did for her, didn't it?

He comes back an hour later with two Spar shopping bags, and as I put away the shopping he reviews the tapes.

"Did good," he says, looking at the computer screen, flickering and lighting his face in a gray glow, his whiskers picked out by the glare. "There'll be no bother if you keep your head screwed on right."

I open the second bag. Everything until now has been what he buys us every week: one chicken, a plastic-wrapped pack of root vegetables, frozen Birds Eye peas, pork sausages, OXO stock cubes, presliced ham, presliced cheese, long-life orange juice, rich tea biscuits, Swan Vesta matches, Mighty White thick-sliced bread, Walkers ready salted multipack, PG Tips tea bags, golden granulated sugar, full-fat milk, margarine, Birds Eye boil-in-the-bag cod in parsley sauce, potatoes, eggs, and frozen pastry. In this bag, under the peas, there's a bottle of Johnson & Johnson wash and shampoo for sensitive skin. Body and hair. I hold up the yellow bottle, hungry to read the ingredients, hungry for new words, to find out what this liquid can do for my child.

"Saw Mary got some dry skin on her legs, under her backside, behind her ears. That stuff will fix it."

He's right. She does have scaly skin, dry patches, some kind of condition on her scalp. I flip the cap and it smells new, soothing, a fresh scent in this same-old-same-old farm cottage.

"Thank you," I say.

"Don't let the bathroom ceiling get too moldy, Jane. Bad for the young'un. You got plenty of paint in the shed, so if it gets sporey again, get up there and fix it, don't wait for me to tell you."

"Okay."

I start preparing dinner. I use the leftover chicken from last night, stripping the carcass, to make a pie. As I pull the delicate oysters from beneath the carcass, I imagine gouging his eyes. As I pull apart the flesh from the wings and thighs, I fantasize about him not being able to fight back. His mother made her pies with sliced carrots and the peas inside the pastry, not on the plate, never on the plate, and she liked to include chopped potato and leftover gravy. He ran through how his mother did things in my early days here. Over and over again. How she folded his shirts. What shade of beige she made his tea and the method she used to bleach the sink. I shred the rest of the meat off the carcass. He took most of yesterday's vegetables for the pigs so I'll use some of the new stuff. I chop and season and fill and spoon and lay the pastry over the top.

There's a loud bang at the front of the house.

Lenn and I walk to the front door and she's smashing the half-cellar door with something, her shoulder, or some tool he keeps down there, and there's dust in the air, floating on the draft from the front door.

I look at him and he runs his fingers over the black bolts.

"Best get the pie in the stove now, Jane."

I retreat to the kitchen and he unlocks the bolts and she screams with some deep guttural voice the tone of which I have never heard. An underground screech. Something Dante might have imagined down in that extra level of hell he never dared to tell us about. The last exhalation of a person in agony. Lenn doesn't say a thing. I can hear her fighting with him, beating down on him, but I know, I know only too well, he is resistant to this. He is hardened to it somehow. From his childhood or from now. A man made from stone. The noises stop and they're down there together. I hear her scream "No!" and then he walks back up the ladder and bolts the door and comes back to the kitchen and sits down at the table.

"When's the tea ready, Jane?"

"Half an hour," I say.

He has beads of sweat in his hairline and there are fresh red scratches on his neck and on his hands.

"I'll have me bath before tea then. Be a good lass and run it for me, would you?"

I run him a hot bath and Huong wakes up. I can feel her wake upstairs in the back bedroom even before I hear her yelps. My milk is hard in my chest. I have a blocked duct, I think.

"I'll go and get her down and feed her by the Rayburn," I say.

"Jane," he says, standing, beckoning me over, placing his hand on my arm, the scratch marks pocked with dried blood. "Been thinkin'. Me mother knew a man in the next village over inland, he were a doctor. When Mary's a bit bigger we could take her to be checked over. You'd have to stay here cuz you're not English, not documented, you ain't legal, but I could take her and say she's a young'un of a worker. Doctor's retired now but he's a local man. He'd see her."

"I want to come with her," I say. "She needs me to be with her."

He chews the inside of his mouth and looks down at the floorboards and back up to me.

"I'll have a think on that," he says. "Maybe you can stay in the Landy when I go in, roped up in the back seat, maybe that'd work alright. But if we're to see a doctor in the next village inland, then you'll need to be no bother between now and then, do you understand me?"

I nod.

"No bother at all, no stepping out of line. I got enough on me plate. And then I'll see what I can do. Maybe we can get out for a little trip, the three of us."

The skies are changing.

From the window in the small back bedroom I watch the sun rise out of the salty waters that I cannot quite see no matter how hard I look, and then during the day when I'm scrubbing and feeding and washing, it tracks around the sky, low, not overhead, and then dips back down, melting into the spires on the horizon with me standing at my front door, back to the half-cellar, watching another day slip away.

There's less washing now. I still have her cloths, her diapers, so many each day. But I've stopped needing the cloths for myself. I'm not sure if he knows or not but he hasn't asked me to take a bath since that night. He hasn't invited me into his front bedroom.

My milk fluctuates. It was plentiful and she was content before, but now, with Huong more hungry than ever, the milk comes and goes. It makes her angry. And then I wonder if she has my anger, a galvanizing, thinking type of anger, or if she has his. I pray to the horizon that she has mine. Or her own.

"Shhh," I say to her. "Settle down."

I want to say *Settle down, Huong*, and I want to say it in my own language but I must be mindful of the camera in the corner of the room. If he hears me speak Vietnamese to her, if he hears her real name, I could lose the letters. Or the Vaseline, or him being more kind, or one day I could lose her altogether. I remember his threat every time I see the long dike. I look at that unending line of still water and my heart collapses in on itself. It's unimaginable. Monstrous. I pull my daughter close and she beats her forehead on my chest. I move her over to the other breast but it is too sore and there's no milk there either. She cries and cries and I rock her and soothe her and kiss her head and I tell her there'll be more milk soon.

When Lenn comes in from drilling winter wheat, I show her to him.

"My milk's dried up," I say. "I have no more milk, very little."

"Me mother fed me till I was four from the teat, it'll be back. And anyway—"

"No," I interrupt him, my voice more firm. "She needs much more than I have, Lenn. She needs some formula, special baby powder we can make into milk. She needs a bottle now, I can't feed her. I don't have what she needs."

"You bother me with this right when I'm back from the fields, on a day like this? Where's me tea?"

"Twenty minutes."

"Better be."

He washes himself and then he shields the keyboard from my vision and he enters his password and he watches the tapes. Most of it in fast-forward mode as always. Tapes of me washing the windows this morning; me making his bed; me feeding Huong in the small back bedroom and reading Kim-Ly's letters; me rushing to the toilet between desperate, failing feeds, my child screaming at me because I'm failing her; me making his tea; me asking for baby formula to keep my child alive. I tried to get into the computer my first week here. Failed password attempt after failed password attempt. I tried Jane and Fen Farm and Gordon and Morecambe and Wise and Lenn and his date of birth. Then the screen locked me out. He tried to burn my pendant necklace for that. And when it didn't burn he took it to the barns in the distance and he fed it to his pigs.

Lenn unbolts the half-cellar door and goes downstairs. I hear nothing. She's been quiet for days, resigned or dead or gagged or injured. Helpless.

He walks back up and locks the door. He drives off to the main yard by the locked halfway gate and then he drives back and walks in with a plastic can.

"Piglet bottle," he says, showing me the object in his hand, the thing with straw stuck to its base with gray mud. "Feeds them alright, do young'un alright and all. Got two sizes of teat: big'un and little'un." He takes two rubber teats from his pocket, one blue and one white. The blue one is coated with something sticky. "See what'll fit her, she's about the size of a little piglet, is Mary."

I look at the bottle. At the dirt. When we had an Argos catalog in the house years ago I knew most of the pages by heart. If you'd asked for a kettle or an ironing board or a three-man tent or a camera, I'd have found the page on the second or third attempt. They had bottles for sale, with sterilizing machines. They were new. Clean. Perfect. They were what babies should have. Not this thing. Huong isn't a piglet for God's sake.

"I need proper formula," I say. "She needs real baby formula, Lenn."

He scratches his head.

"Ain't nothing can be done about that. Ain't like I can go waltzing down to the Spar shop and ask for baby formula now, is it? I mean, come on. Sue or Larry would say, 'Now then, Leonard, what on God's green earth you be wanting with baby formula?' I ain't asking for it, Jane. Nothin' for it. Young'un will have good old cow's milk from the bottle just like the rest of us and then she'll be fine, grow up strong as her mother."

"Give me those," I say, taking the bottle, the enormous, agricultural, filthy, awful bottle, and the two dirty rubber teats. I run the hot water in the kitchen sink and scrub the bottle inside and out and scrub the teats and rinse the detergent off and rinse them again and then dry them with clean towels. Then I wash them all over again to make sure. I take the milk from the fridge and warm it in his mother's saucepan until it's at about body temperature. I fill the bottle one-eighth full and screw on the big rubber teat.

"Don't give the baby that!"

I look down at my feet, at the voice, at the floorboards.

"Why not?" I say back, my first words to her.

Lenn stamps on the floor and the room shakes.

"Why not?" I yell.

He runs to the door of the half-cellar and unbolts it and she's screaming to me something about the baby not drinking cow's milk, about allergies, how it can be dangerous, but he's reached her and she's crying and then the door's bolted shut again and Lenn's in front of me, his gray hair loose across his bulging eyes.

"Get the young'un and bring her down here. Get the letters and all."

I shake my head. "Lenn, please."

"I said get 'em."

I drag myself up the stairs, my heart pounding in my chest. Huong's asleep where I left her. I pick her up and she wakes and moves her head close to my breast and latches on and I let her, the little good it will do her. She bangs her head against my chest in frustration as I shuffle downstairs.

"Give her a feed then no more bother."

I take the bottle, as big as a family-size milk carton from a super-market. I sit on the sofa and my eyes flood with tears and the tears fall onto her perfect face as I try to guide the rubber teat of the pig-let bottle into her perfect mouth. She won't take it. She wants me, wants my milk, my touch; she doesn't want this thing he's brought me. I try to feed her from myself but there's nothing. I cover my chest and try again with the bottle and the white teat and she yells until her tears mix with mine, hers full of salt, mine empty and hopeless and stale.

"Mary will take it," says Lenn, watching from the Rayburn. "She'll get hungry enough and then she'll take it, mark my words."

She doesn't. She just shrieks and yells and cries and looks at me, right at me.

Lenn wants his tea now so I put her down on the sofa, the noise deafening; and my ears, my foot, my back, my skin, all hurting, my heart as bruised as it has ever been, and I fry his eggs and his ham in his mother's skillet the way she used to do it.

"Frost in the air," says Lenn, finishing the last on his plate. "Be red sky in mornin', mark my words."

I clear the table and try Huong with the bottle once more. I even suck from it myself to show her. She refuses. She works herself up into a state where she's blotchy and then she throws up what little milk is in her stomach and she gasps and cries. Her body is losing its softness. Her head's starting to look too big on her body. I give her my breast to settle her, and it does, but she is so hungry it makes me livid.

"Here, have this, settle yourself down." He passes me a fragment of a horse pill, one-quarter. I've started taking this sometimes, a top-up before bed to soothe me to sleep. Otherwise I can't cope. And I must cope, I do not have a choice, it's this or nothing.

He unlocks the corner cabinet and turns on the TV. Local news. I see the fear in his eyes as the newsreader mentions a missing woman, Cynthia Townsend. He steps over toward the corner of the room, closer to the TV, and shields the screen with his bulk. The story runs for thirty seconds, maybe less, but he is affected. Lenn walks back to his armchair and sits heavily. He glances down to the floorboards and then he beckons me over.

Could this be our way out? The police finding us all here? Helping us?

We watch a Grand Prix race. The same lap over and over and over again like every day of my life. The race is taking place in Malaysia and even though it doesn't look like home, and the people dress differently and the light isn't the same, the vegetation looks familiar. I stare at the trees. Huong takes the bottle in the end even though I can tell that she hates it and she would tell me if she could, she would kick the back of my knees in protest if she could. I sit there feeding her from this unwieldy bottle with him behind me, his bloodied cuticles tangling in my hair, his dry palm on my scalp, and Cynth right underneath me. She's silent but I can sense her down there, bent double, wasting away. All hope receding. He took the leftovers down along with a bucket of water like he does every night. And he brings a bucket back up and empties it on the other side of the shed, or sometimes straight into the septic tank he built himself as a young man. She's down there listening to us right now. She's giving up, she must be.

When the race is over he helps me to my feet and we make our way upstairs. He says, "'Night then, sleep tight, you and the young'un," and then he takes a thin cotton sheet and a small towel from his mother's linen closet, and he folds them under his arm, and he heads downstairs.

18

Little Huong's getting worse.

It started with her crying at night, with Lenn telling me to shut her up, and now she has fallen quiet but she's vomiting the cow's milk up as soon as I give it to her.

She's pale and gaunt. Babies shouldn't look gaunt. Her skin is graying. I watch the pulse in her neck.

I can't give her bread or rich tea biscuits; he keeps telling me to try it, to soften them first in my mouth like a bird in a nest up in a tree, but she is too young for it. The crumbs of the one rich tea I did give her, she vomited back up at me with a look in her eyes like *Mother, why are you doing this to me, why can't you help me?*

Is she allergic to cow's milk or just too young for it? I would give a kidney right now, a kidney and one of my eyes and one of my hands for just ten minutes with a proper doctor. I would give more. Just to check her over and listen to her heart and her lungs, to run tests, take blood, to tell me what to do, to say, *Your daughter will survive.*

Part of me wants to ask him to search for baby digestive problems on the computer. But the other part knows I must retain as much goodwill as possible. If she gets worse I need to know I haven't used up my favors too early.

I get his lunch ready, peeling each presliced slice of mild cheddar from its neighbor, sitting it on the margarine slurry on the thick-cut Mighty White bread, closing it up. Back home we had *bánh mì,* baguettes sliced and filled with grilled pork, the fat caramelized and crisp, with bright green coriander and peppers. They were delicious, and this is as far as it is possible to be from that. Huong's asleep on the sofa and her cheeks are not red like they used to be.

"Landy needs new tires, two new ones I reckon, back end, bald as eggs, ain't gonna make it through winter with tires like them back'uns."

"Lenn."

He looks at me, his sandwich small in his oil-greased hand.

"She still won't eat."

He takes a bite of his Mighty White sandwich and looks at her lying on the plastic-wrapped sofa, her neck to one side, her pulse clearly visible below her jawline.

"Mary'll get the hang of it, just give it time."

"There's been blood in her diapers, Lenn. She's vomiting the cow's milk back up. She can't keep it down."

He looks back to me.

"Blood?"

I nod.

"From the rash?"

I shake my head.

He sniffs and wipes his nose with his sleeve.

"I can't just waltz into the Spar shop in the village and ask for two tins of formula for the young'un, now can I? You see what I mean, I can't just go in and say it, can I?"

"Could you buy it somewhere else, Lenn? Could you drive a little farther, to a bigger town where they don't know who you are? Could you do that and buy a few weeks' worth, it'd be no bother, nobody would know."

He looks out of the window as if to think of what towns lie out there and in what direction.

Say yes, you foul man. Grant me this one thing.

"You mean so you can try and leave here with the young'un, is that it? That's what's in your head, is it? Me gone for an hour or more to town past the bridge and then you go up the track with your busted foot carryin' me young'un and then you try and get out of here, is that it?"

I shake my head.

"She'll die, Lenn."

He looks at her and swallows his mouthful and takes another bite.

"I'll think on it this afternoon and tell you tonight. Ain't gonna be so easy as you reckon, you got no experience of these things, not in England."

"Thank you."

That's as good as I can hope for. Better, even. I know when to stop and shut up. I have learned how to survive with this creature and at what point to back down, even though it makes me rage inside to admit it.

He walks to the door and the phone bolted to the floor rings and we both freeze. It rings and Huong wakes up on the sofa and there's a yell from beneath us, a feral cry, and Lenn stamps his foot and both Huong and Cynth fall silent.

He leaves.

I take Huong and try to feed her from my breast but there is nothing and she just gets agitated there. I thought it'd comfort her, me being with her, close to her, the warmth, the familiar scent, but she gets angry and her wrists don't feel like they did a week ago, they've lost the fat ring below the hand, they've lost their innocence. They're miniature adult hands now.

So I take the wretched piglet bottle. And the teat, the blue one, it works the best. And I warm the milk on the Rayburn and pour it in and check the temperature on my tongue, on my hand, on my upper lip. She takes it. She sucks and throws her arms around it like it's a fresh new mother and she sucks it down. But then she vomits and cries. Her tears don't spray anymore, they just fall. They roll down her cheeks without the energy needed to fly. They're adult tears now, and sick adult tears at that.

I feel warmth on my arm and drag the cloths out from under the sofa and open her diaper. Liquid. She's had diarrhea for days. What little milk she keeps down just passes straight through her.

"I'm sorry," I whisper. "You'll be okay little one, we'll get you some food soon, I promise, you'll be alright. Stay with me, Huong. Stay strong a little longer."

I clean her up with paper towels and water and throw the cloth diaper into the washing machine. Thank God for the Vaseline, she needs it every day now.

Staring out of the kitchen window, I see him drive off toward his precious pigs.

There's a noise.

I crouch down and look at the kitchen cabinets and it sounds like a snake from my grandparents' garden hissing up at me.

Huong's gurgling on the sofa. I look over at her and then back down to the floor. Hissing and tapping. Something metallic. I crouch but it's too much for my ankle so I get down on the floor and the hiss is there and I open the cabinet under the kitchen sink.

There's a bucket moving. The bucket I use to mop the floors, it's rocking by itself. I move it and it's replaced by the dirtiest fingertip I have ever seen.

I look at it.

And then I reach in and touch it with my own finger and I can hear crying from below me, directly under me, Cynth sobbing and the soft pads of our fingertips—mine clean, hers almost black with grime—touching, connected.

She pulls her finger back down and whispers through the hole. "Thank you."

I almost die from the guilt.

She's thanking me for what, for meeting her fingertip with my own? After these weeks of me not helping her, not letting her out, not risking my daughter's life to come to her aid? She's thanking me for that?

"I'm coming back," I whisper. "Wait there."

I grip the cabinet door and then grab the porcelain lip of the sink and heave myself upright and then I find his plate. He left one edge of one mild cheddar sandwich. I clear the plate into the sink like I always do and then, with my back to the camera in the corner of the room, watching me, listening, I crouch again. I must be quick.

I shred the edge of the sandwich into thin strips and pass down the first strip, mainly crust, into the hole and it's taken from me like there's a piranha down there. I feed it all through and then I say, "I'll be back when I can, I'll do what I can."

"Thank you," she whispers.

I shake my head with the awful shame of it all and then I take Huong in my arms and wrap her in blankets and take her outside for some air.

The day is bright and clear.

There are clouds sitting in the air like balloons, their lower edges gray and flat, their tops like cushions in a rich man's house. I show

Huong every corner of the compass, the spires to the north and the wind turbines to the south and the flatness sloping down to the salt marshes past the pig barn in the east and the tiny specks passing one another on the flat roads to the west. Some color comes back to her cheeks, but her wrists are still thin.

I squeeze her hands. I feel her feet through the blanket. I place my palm to her forehead. Desperate, useless measures to judge her health. Her ill health.

I think it's a plane but I know it's not. And it's not a bird, I know all the birds that fly these fens and it is not one of them. It's something in between. Humming across the sky like an overgrown insect, some kind of fan at its back, like a hang glider with an engine. Not as high as a plane, not as low as a bird, somewhere in between. I want to scream, to burn this house down to the ground to show it where I am, to plead for the pilot to pick us up, me and Huong and Cynth, and take off with us, away past the horizon to somewhere safe.

But I just watch it fly on by, humming, buzzing.

I tried to burn the cottage down once before in the early days.

It was after my ankle, maybe six months later, at my lowest point. I took the box of Swan Vestas upstairs and lit some scrunched pages of newspaper in the corner of his front bedroom. I burned the sheet he made me lie under, the old one. But Lenn saw. He was out on his tractor drilling for that year's cabbages and he saw the smoke and he came back to the house and put it out. A farmer in fenland can see all of his land wherever he is. I lost my passport that time. And I had to repaint the bedroom even though I could hardly stand up. I had to repaint it eleven times to cover the smoke marks.

Tonight is sausage and mashed potatoes night. I don't mind it. This time it needs to be good, needs to be absolutely perfect so he'll agree to buying Huong some baby formula tomorrow, she can't wait much longer. I cannot put a foot wrong. Soon she'll need a drip, medicine, a doctor, a team of doctors, intensive care.

Huong has to be my priority but I'm not failing Cynth. I'll make sure my daughter lives, and then I will make sure Cynth lives. I can do both things.

My focus is unwavering. Like a fighter pilot or a watchmaker. The sausages must be just like his mother fried them. They cannot deviate from the exacting standards he has laid down.

I warm the skillet on the hot plate.

I fry the sausages the way he likes them as he watches the tapes. My back is as straight as a fence post, my ears alert to his every huff and puff. Will he see my whispers to Cynth beneath the sink? Will he sense what I was doing?

"Been thinkin' on what you said earlier about that shop in the big town over yonder, past the bridge."

I look at him. Please. I will do anything you ask, she needs food or she will die. I beg you.

"Reckon I can do it this comin' weekend most likely."

I shake my head, must stay calm, must keep frying his damn sausages the way his mother used to fry them in his mother's cast-iron skillet. I cannot burn them too black or let them split in the wrong way.

"She won't make it, Lenn. She's too weak now. She needs it tomorrow. Please."

He looks at the sausages hissing and spitting in the pan. He looks at me and then he looks at Huong and she's curled on the plastic dust sheet on the sofa, asleep.

"Tomorrow, then."

I feel like kissing him. I feel like letting go of this pan and this stove and falling at his size eleven feet.

"Thank you," I say, keeping the browning of the sausages as even as I can.

We eat in silence.

"Them was good sausages," he says. "I'm goin' down to the pigs with the scraps bucket."

I want to say, *Why don't you give them to Cynth for God's sake? Why don't you give her half?* But I say nothing. I have to secure the formula first. I have to do nothing, not one thing, to sabotage this plan. I have to tread silently and say nothing and do nothing. Just one more day.

He leaves and moments later I hear a hiss again from beneath my feet. I close my eyes and bite my lips inside my mouth and collect Huong and her piglet milk bottle and take her upstairs. The hissing is still there behind me, along with the tapping under the bucket, the quiet pleading ignored, the woman forgotten, the mother and child away.

When I wake up, the horse pills thick in my head, she feels cold.

I pull her to my chest and wrap sheets and blankets around us. I rub her back, the thin skin covering her spine, the bumps of each vertebra, the butterfly wings of her shoulder blades that feel like they're sharpening hour by hour. I breathe on her face. I give her all the warmth I have but she is still cool. Cool and pale and slow in her eyes.

I inch downstairs on my backside and put more willow on the fire. I load it full and then squeeze in a twisted knotty log and fasten the fire door. Then I run her a bath, a little deeper than usual, a little warmer than usual. The water is fine but the room is cold and wet, spores along the ceiling, creeping webs of mold climbing up the walls, the floor spongy under my feet. I lower her into the bath. She doesn't flinch or scream, she doesn't look straight at me like she normally does, her lips are more purple than red. I run more hot water, using my hand to shield her from any scalding drops.

"Huong," I whisper. "He's going today. He'll get you new food today, proper baby food." I splash the water on her body, more hot from the faucet, more warmth. "You'll be okay, my darling. You must stay strong. There will be baby milk for dinner, proper milk just for you."

She stares up with blank eyes.

She doesn't react to the drops of water that fall near her face. She doesn't even blink.

I take her out to the Rayburn and dry her in one of his mother's threadbare towels. I've opened the fire door. She seems to look at the flames, the orange and the yellow licking her pupils as I gaze at her with worry and love and terror and hope.

She's warm now.

But she is not screaming and that's the worst thing of all. She is silent. Hungry. And so is Cynth.

Lenn comes in as I'm preparing the cow's milk. I loathe it and I never want to see it ever again. The bottle, the piglet feeding bottle, is drying on the warm area near the stove.

"Might be tomorrow, me gettin' off to that big shop in town over yonder past the bridge, ain't sure one way or the other yet."

"No," I say, my hands shaking with rage. With fear. "Lenn, look at her, she won't make it."

"I'm lookin'," he says. "And she looks right as rain. Don't go naggin' me, Jane, I'll do it when I can do it."

"Your daughter"—I say, but she is not his daughter, she will never be his daughter, no relation whatsoever—"will die in the night." I say this with the certainty of a priest or a politician.

He looks at her again and sniffs.

My heart is throbbing with anger. With terror.

"I'll maybe get off after me sandwich, ain't makin' no promises, mind you."

I mouth *thank you* without saying it because I want his words to be the last spoken, as if that lends them permanence and weight, as if that will make them come true.

Lenn takes down the medicine bottle from the top of the cabinet and unscrews the big metal lid and removes three fragments and puts them down on the pine table.

I nod to him and bow my head.

While he eats his sandwich I feed Huong from the big plastic piglet bottle. She doesn't suck. I move the teat around, the blue one, and try to squeeze the bottle a little, but she won't take it and she won't look me in the eye and I could give up right now. She has turned her face away from me. If she passes now it will be with one infant thought, one clear and untainted opinion: that her own mother failed her. I had one job. I try to move her to the other side, a cushion under my arm, tempting her with the synthetic teat, but she won't latch on.

"Please, darling. Drink," I say, my voice catching in my mouth. "Please, just a little. Take a sip."

She opens her mouth and I gently push in the teat and I think she tries to suckle, some reflex coming back to life, but then the milk just pours out of her mouth and she coughs and I pat her back and she feels loose in my arms.

I turn to face Lenn and he sees the haunting in my eyes and he leaves immediately.

I watch his Land Rover drive away, faster than he normally drives, water spraying up from the puddles on the track. I hold her to me. He unlocks the halfway gate and drives through and relocks it and drives away.

He's gone and I want him back in minutes. For the first time in my life I want him to come home.

I take Huong over to the Rayburn to keep her warm and I bring my washcloths and a bucket and some soap. I crouch down onto the floor by the sink and open the cabinet. The bucket is steady. I move it aside and hiss like she does; I have Huong in the crook of my arm, she's asleep now, and I poke my finger down into the hole.

Nothing.

I hiss and hiss and poke my finger in and out of that hole in the floorboard and finally something touches my fingertip and pushes me back up to this level. I watch her nail, long and filthy, rise through the floor in my under-sink cabinet.

"I need help," I say.

"*I* need help," she says.

"My baby is sick. She won't take the cow's milk."

"Is she conscious?" she asks.

"Yes."

"Feed her a little at a time, drip it from your finger. Or dab it on your nipple. Add some sugar to the milk. Make sure it's warm. Just drops will keep her with you until he gets back with formula. Give her a drop of water too. Keep her warm."

I push a one-third fragment of a horse pill down through the hole.

"What is it?" she whispers.

"A tablet for the pain," I say.

She says nothing.

"Thank you," I say. "You have helped me."

"Save your child," she says. "And then save me."

She sticks her finger up through the hole again and I take it between my thumb and forefinger and I shake it and then I bend to get my head inside the cabinet and I kiss it.

Lenn comes back within the hour.

He drives like a maniac up the track and I have the fire stoked and the piglet bottle washed, ready for Huong's powdered milk. Her medicine.

I open the front door and he runs from the Land Rover carrying Tesco bags.

"She alright?" he says.

"Give it to me," I say.

He upends both bags onto the plastic-wrapped sofa and I could hug him.

He hands me a large cylindrical tub of baby formula and I open it and there's a plastic scoop in there and I read the instructions as quickly as I can, and he hands me a new bottle, fresh, not for piglets but for human babies, and I dunk it into the water boiling on the stove and shake it to dry it off. She's slipping, I can feel it. She looks the same but she's giving up.

I make up the bottle and shake it and squeeze it onto my wrist and it's too hot. But I can't wait any longer. I cradle her in my arm and she weighs less than a pillowcase. I push the nipple, a proper purpose-built baby nipple of the correct size, to her mouth.

She won't take it.

"Please," I say.

"Give her a minute," says Lenn.

I let a drip fall onto her lips. She won't suckle. I spoon a little into her mouth and she vomits it back out.

"Lenn, we need a doctor now. It's been too long. We need help."

"Rubbish. She'll be alright, will Mary. Besides, there's people out there lookin', I know there is." He glances down at the floorboards. "Posters up in show windows. Ain't safe. Just keep on at it and Mary will take it if she knows what's good for her."

I am desperate. Exhausted. I want Cynth up here and the midwife I never had and the mother I've not seen for nine years and my sister and a pediatrician. All I have is him.

With the back of my hand I stroke her and she looks at me. Her eyes, her lashes, my sister's lashes. She opens her mouth and takes the nipple. She doesn't suckle much, just a few seconds, but she takes in some of the milk and it stays down. I look at Lenn and he looks away and sighs and rubs his head.

She sleeps after her feed. I place her down and she's still as pale as bone but she seems content. He bought us two bottles, each with a nipple, and about a three months' supply of powdered baby formula. And a rabbit. He bought Huong a soft rabbit, pale blue, called Tommy. He didn't have to do that but he did.

I heat his boil-in-the-bag cod in parsley sauce in a pan. I boil his potatoes and his frozen peas. I take real care over every detail because of that rabbit. I want him to eat well tonight, to enjoy his dinner, because he saved my daughter's life and he bought her a toy.

He goes off on his quad to feed his pigs.

Huong's asleep on the sofa.

I go outside.

The air is thick with woodsmoke and frost and the birds are hanging in the still air like flies trapped in some otherworldly cobweb. I hobble around to the rear of the house, to his homemade bathroom extension, and stretch up to the place where the wall meets the roof and there's a gap just beneath, perhaps a frost crack in between the cinder blocks from before they were laid, and I pull out an orange hard candy. Lenn calls them "car candy." I've never eaten one in a car. It's chipped and dusty and there's something dead stuck underneath it, a tiny red spider, but it's still edible.

I check that Lenn's still out at the pig barn and then I go back inside and check Huong and then I open the cabinet under the sink. I move the bucket and hiss and hiss and hiss. Huong wakes up and yells. Such beautiful sounds. Loud. More vibrant than in days. The blackened finger pokes up and I place the orange hard candy in the hole and then I push it down and it can hardly squeeze through. I twist it and push and it drops down to her.

"God bless you," she says.

20

We've had a few good days.

It took time for Huong to take the bottle, to drink the formula and keep it down. I had to start with excruciatingly small feeds. The volume she could ingest, the minuteness of it, pained me. Huong's stomach must have been shrunken to the size of an almond. But her heat came back soon enough, and her color. She's eager for the new bottle, a real bottle, the nipple of which was designed for her perfect mouth and not the mouth of an infant swine.

He's left us to it pretty much. I keep up with my chores and make sure his eggs are fried right, flipped, not too brown underneath, never broken, ever, always runny. Not easy on a wood-burning Rayburn. It's getting the fire right, at the correct time, planning it all, placing the skillet in the correct place on the hot plate, judging the zones of the pan, that's the trick.

I'm lying here with my good foot off the bed and my bad foot resting at some awful angle. I'm starting to lose sensation in it. This is a godsend as the pain is migrating away from me along with the feeling, but I remember when this happened to my uncle. He lost the sensation in one leg. Pins and needles. It was dying. The doctors had to cut it off. He was in a good hospital but he still died soon after. Sepsis.

She's asleep on my arm.

Her hair, her dark, perfect hair, is starting to curl a little like his does. I run my fingertips through it as she purrs her deep baby sleep, nestled in the crook of my arm, her stomach full. The diarrhea has stopped and the blood has stopped. She still vomits if I feed her too much in one sitting, but I'm so eager to build her up so that one day she can flee this place and then I'll have done something good with my life. My sister may have been sent back but Huong will have a full life in this country, I'll give her everything she needs, all the lessons, all the self-confidence and strength, and then I'll set her free. Maybe she'll get word to someone in time to save me or maybe that won't be possible. It has no relevance. She'll be away from this cottage one day. Nine, ten years from now. Running down the road with a message and that banknote I keep behind the storage heater in the back bedroom. I smile at the idea. Her leaving. That's my rabbits and my alfalfa right there.

I sleep and she wakes me and I take her down for a bottle.

She smiles.

This is a new thing, the most miraculous new thing, miraculous for any baby, but especially for Huong. She's happy. She looks at me and, even though she lives here, she smiles right into my eyes. My daughter is healthy and calm.

"Goin' down to feed the pigs early tonight before them fireworks start settin' off."

I frown at Lenn as he removes his jacket and hangs it next to the locked key box.

"Fireworks night, ain't it? Gunpowder, treason, and plot. Idiots spendin' money they don't have more like it. Pigs don't like it, makes them frit."

Makes *them* frit? What if I'm frit? What if my daughter's frit? What if—I look down to my feet—what if she's frit down there? He's worried his pigs are frit?

"Ain't checkin' the tapes tonight," he says. "Have me food on the table when I get in."

I don't believe him.

He will check the tapes.

But I need to get a fragment—the fragment I skipped—I need to get it down to her. I haven't contacted her these past three days partly because it'll look suspicious me cleaning out the cabinet under the sink every day, and partly because I needed the full three-quarter dose. Every fourth day he gives me the fragments and I give her one of them. I'm not sure if it helps her but it's something. I've managed to get some cold fries through the hole to her, a rolled-up slice of ham, some mild cheddar, more crusts. She's alive down there but she's stopped making any noises. No sobbing, no pleading, no crying. She doesn't even hiss anymore, just taps the bucket. I can't imagine it. Crouched or lying, no bath, no toilet, just a bucket, one with scraps he takes down and one with her waste he brings up. No light. No change of clothes. How will she ever see again? Will she die down there with no light?

I am being forced to play Russian roulette on this fen. Maybe that's a poor example; it's like the universe is saying *I'll shoot your mother or your father. If you don't choose one I'll shoot them both. Now make your choice.*

Except this is worse because in a way the decision has been made for me. If I help her too much, I risk my child. If I focus on Huong too much and don't take any risks, Cynth will surely die. Or worse, she'll just suffer on and on indefinitely. I understand how microscopic kindnesses—warm words and rolled-up slices of ham—can buy a soul a few more weeks. His rare kindnesses, even though they're shrouded in something unspeakably cruel, keep me moving forward.

I hear a bang.

Through the window I can see a light in the sky, some reds and yellows over by the wind turbines. They're early. Just kids. Back home we'd have mesmerizing fireworks—dazzling colors, whizzes and bangs and crackles—and we'd be together to watch them and we'd smile and hold hands and smell the gunpowder in the warm evening air.

I stick a log in the firebox of the Rayburn and slide the broth onto the hot plate. Translucent globules of fat move around on the surface. When will Huong be able to take a sip? Or a nibble of a mushed carrot? Next spring? I have nobody to tell me the answers, no parenting books, certainly not Lenn. I must feel my way through this on my own.

I pick up Huong from the plastic-wrapped sofa and she blinks at me. We stand at the sink. The bucket rattles, I can just about hear it. I pretend to drop Huong's feeding cloth and then we crouch down, her in my arms, and I open the cabinet door. He will watch the tapes, I know he will, I must be quick. I move the bucket. Her finger. Like a blackened root sticking up through the soil from underground. The world corrupted. Nature reversed. I touch the finger quickly and take the fragment of horse pill from the pocket in his mother's apron and pass it down the hole to her. She puts her grimy fingertip back through. What else does she need? What else can I give her? She needs more. And then Huong moves her foot. I lift my child toward the probing finger. I position her cheek, now recovering some of its chubbiness, over the hole and lower her gently and Cynth, the woman under this blackened finger, she strokes my daughter's plump cheek. I hear sobs down there. In my head she is smiling, her trembling fingertip caressing fresh skin, pure and clean and fat, new, an ally, a friend, a child, an innocent. She sobs and then she whispers.

"God bless you, child. And you, Jane."

I pull Huong back up and touch the fingertip with my own and then I try to move the bucket back but she won't withdraw her finger. He'll be back soon. I nudge the finger with the bucket a few times and she pulls it down reluctantly, slowly, the digit half bent with resignation, and I place the bucket back in its place and close the door and pray to the horizon that my daughter's cheek has bought Cynth more time.

Lenn comes back and we eat the broth. Back home I'd add a dozen herbs and spices—coriander and mint, handfuls of each; basil and chilies and ginger and cloves and star anise—and noodles and limes and it would be a thing of beautiful sustenance. But this is okay. It's still stock, the basic foundation, and I add plenty of cracked black pepper to mine.

He slurps from his spoon. A strand of carrot lies across his lip. He's been jittery ever since he found out the police are searching for Cynth. He's not used to that. There was never anybody out there searching for me like they are for her.

I give Huong a feed, she can take a little more now, and then I stoke up the Rayburn until the thermometer gauge is at the maximum.

"Let's have a look at them rockets," says Lenn.

So instead of unlocking the TV cabinet, he opens the front door. And instead of watching snooker or the news, we look out at the land, his land. We stand on the doorstep together like a real couple with heat at our backs and cold on our faces. Huong's asleep, satisfied. Cynth's had her horse pill fragment and I hope that affords her some relief, some short-lived escape.

The colors intensify, lighting the undersides of clouds and giving a golden fringe to the trees and steeples in the distance. I watch lights soar into the sky and then there's a pause, a sweet expectation, and the thing explodes into a thousand sparks and then the noise arrives here at this miserable flatland farm.

They last for half an hour. Huong sleeps through it, her backside smooth and Vaselined, her stomach full.

"Get up to bed," says Lenn. "Nothin' good on TV tonight anyway."

I take her up.

When she's asleep on me and I'm reading my sister's fifth letter, the paper crumpled and grubby at the edges from all the times I've handled it over the years, Lenn comes upstairs and looks in on us both and then he smiles and takes the thin cotton sheet and the small towel and heads down to the half-cellar.

I try not to think of it, what good can come of that?

There is no noise.

I reread Kim-Ly's letter, her words of hope, of survival. She tells me about her friendly new boss at the nail salon, and I'm absurdly hopeful even though I know full well the boss turns out to be a vicious thief and even though I know this boss gets deported sometime between letter twenty-eight and twenty-nine and even though I know Kim-Ly is back in Vietnam with her debt still to pay off. I try to focus on what she tells me she sees from her shared bedroom window. A fox. More gray than orange. It comes back night after night, and she thinks it lives under a neighbor's garden shed. I try to flood myself with Kim-Ly's words to exorcise the thoughts I have of what's happening right now in the hell that is one-and-a-half floors beneath me.

Huong sleeps with her clammy palm on my breast. Her wrists are slowly coming back. I think they're turning from adult wrists back to baby wrists again. The safety buffer is returning under her skin.

There's a slam downstairs. Bolts being secured. Footsteps. The stairs. I bring Huong closer to me, folding my arms around her, building a wall in front of her with my body.

"What the hell do you call this?"

He's holding out his big open palm in the doorframe to the small back bedroom. I can see a collection, maybe three, maybe five, grimy fragments of horse pill.

"Lenn, I . . ."

"Get up off your backside."

She's been saving them? For what? Why didn't she help herself?

"Downstairs."

He points down.

I shuffle to the top of the stairs and look at him and sit down on the top step and start to move down one at a time.

Cynth was saving them up. She was going to kill herself down there with the grimy fragments. She'd need three whole pills I think, nine fragments. I'd need at least four. She almost did it. She almost escaped all this.

He points to the half-cellar door and I walk, Huong cradled in my arms, a blanket over her.

"Maybe I'll put you and Mary down with her for a few weeks, down in the cellar, no bottles or nothin', would that make things clearer to you?"

He starts unbolting the top bolt.

"No," I say. "Lenn, no, Mary can't. Not down there."

"Just you then, is it? Leave the young'un with me up here and you go down with your friend for a bit, shall we?"

"Please, Lenn," I say. "I'm sorry. I'm so sorry, I thought she was in pain, that's all."

"Bring me them letters and you're lucky I won't stick you and the young'un both down there with her."

I look at him. My eyes say: Have some mercy. My eyes say: The letters are all I have left, they are my one remaining possession, they are my family and my roots and my anchor. My mouth says: "Okay."

21

I inch up the stairs, my ankle—limp, swollen, mangled—dragging behind me.

The back bedroom storage closet smells of his mother. Even though I never met the woman I know exactly, with the precision of a master perfumer, what her smells were. Are. They still live on here. And with every possession of mine that he burns in the Rayburn the smell of her intensifies and the smell of me fades. Her things remain whereas mine end up as ash on the pile outside by the septic tank. On the right side of the closet are neat stacks of her things. Neat because I wash them and press them and stack them. Petticoats I don't wear and cloths I use for Huong and will probably have to start to use myself again soon. Towels as thin and as rough as old rugs. Aprons. Jumpers with moth holes and skirts made from thick cloth and stockings I've never tried on and a hat and a pair of gloves I sometimes use in the wintertime. It all smells overwhelmingly of Jane, his mother. He never speaks of her funeral or where she's buried. If she rests in a local village churchyard or somewhere on the farm. On the other side of the closet are six identical wooden shelves. On the third shelf is a twine-bound stack of letters. Hand-written. Undated. Two years' worth of Kim-Ly's thoughts and dreams and musings and observations; memories of our mother and our school days. These are mine. Panic surges in my chest. My one last thing. He will surely burn them today, but when they are cinders flying up through the kinked chimney breast up to the sky, when they are reduced to ashes in the garden, they will still be mine.

I pick them up and hold them to my nose.

At the bottom of the stairs I hand them over to him. I haven't looked at them and I haven't sneaked one out because he will know. I can't make any mistakes from now on. No micro-rebellions. I have no bargaining chips left, nothing to lose except her, nothing to cling to. Zero physical possessions of my own. I have nothing.

Last week I had a nightmare. His eggs were cooked for too long, the yolks had turned hard. I woke from that terror at the moment before he pushed Huong into the Rayburn firebox. The sensation of terror in my bones has never felt more intense. It was so powerful it changed me.

He takes the letters and flicks through them like a bank robber in a film might flick through a stack of dollar bills. He looks at me and then he opens the Rayburn fire door. It's quiet in there, just embers.

"Have to behave yourself now, won't you?"

I make my eyes as empty as I can and then I nod.

"Mind you do, then," he says.

Lenn jabs the stack of letters, curling in his hand, at Huong. He points at my daughter with her own aunt's letters. Then he flings them in the embers.

They sit there for a few moments. Curling. Blackening. I could reach in and take them if I were stronger, braver, more stupid. Take them and then beat him with the poker. But I watch. He watches too. The whole stack takes at the same time, a flame springing up from beneath them, from some incendiary point, some random heat spot, and it takes them and holds them. The brightness fills the room. Seventy-two handwritten letters from my own baby sister. Tens of thousands of her words. Huong moves her arm so it rests against the skin of my clavicle and she comforts me. It is I who should look after her but at this moment, on this farm, his farm, with the flames licking the outer door of the Rayburn, it's she who sustains me. Her touch. The potential in her tiny body, the possibilities contained inside of her. She comforts me and I take it.

"That's that, then," says Lenn, walking to the bathroom and closing the door behind him, something I've not been allowed to do for seven years, closing that door and making it a room.

The flames die away and turn amber-red. To my left and to my right, through the windows, I can see sparks and cascades in the huge fenland skies. Hazy fireworks in my peripheral vision. The booms are subdued but the lights are everywhere tonight. I pray to the horizon to keep Kim-Ly and Huong and Cynth safe, to keep them themselves.

The next day I wake and feel empty.

What can I rely on now that the last scrap of my identity has been destroyed? Huong? It's too heavy a burden for her to carry. Too unwieldy. For her to be the only reference point of life, my only hint of goodness, it seems unfair. And yet she gazes up at me after her morning feed and smiles and she looks like new light.

Downstairs, he's under the kitchen sink.

"Mouse holes," he says, looking up at me. "Old'uns. Little rats used to scurry up and down. Hole here under the bucket, but I expect you know full well all about it, don't you?"

He screws up tinfoil into a ball. He compresses it inside his massive fist and adds another sheet and compresses it and then he pushes it down into the hole. He places a piece of pine over the top and screws it down onto the floorboards with eight screws.

"That'll do her."

He spends the day on the winter wheat and on cleaning out the old combine. By the time I see him driving back to the locked halfway gate, there are mists all over the land. They're layered like stripes, like white animal hairs floating horizontally in front of the distance, each one almost see-through, each one straight and whisper thin.

We eat ham, eggs, and fries. He says it's alright. All I can think about is if Cynth is getting enough air down there now that the under-sink hole is completely sealed over. She'll be relying on whatever oxygen slips through under and around the bolted door, so I must keep the front door open during the day regardless of the chill, must keep the air flowing in. I dreamed I passed her down a pair of knitting needles and a ball of wool, pushing the fabric down, her pulling one end and balling it up down there in the dark. She could have made herself a sweater. Because it's very cold now and I'm not sure how she's still alive down there in the dark, not being able to stand upright, him going down to her whenever he feels like it.

Dessert is bananas and custard. A treat. He does this from time to time, brings in another dish, like the pineapple, or once it was a sponge pudding. I heat the ready-made custard on the hot plate and it looks like egg yolks mixed with bright yellow paint. I slice two bananas into the goop and serve it up in two of his mother's bowls.

"It's not bad, is it?"

It's delicious. I eat it and I dip my little finger into the tepid custard when I'm almost done and I let Huong lick the sweetness from me. She likes it. She smiles and wrinkles her nose like this is the best day of her life so far. Like she's lucky to be alive.

"Young'un be learnin' from you soon, I expect," he says. "How to peel carrots and taters and how to scrub the sink and scrub floors and that."

No.

Huong will be a pilot or an engineer or a teacher or a nurse or a factory worker or a professor or an artist or a priest. She will not become me. I will not allow it.

We watch *Match of the Day*. Lenn sits heavy in his armchair with his hand on my head and I sit on the floor wondering how Cynth is managing directly beneath me. I want to pass her something, a message, a piece of bread.

"Not bad, is it, really?" says Lenn. "You and me and young'un, a good hot fire, football on the TV, a roof over our heads, it's alright, ain't it?"

I look down at Huong. She's asleep in my arms, her eyelashes fluttering through a dream. Keep dreaming, my darling. Anything but here. Dream of a savanna and of family walks through a forest, dream of playing with your future friends in Saigon and of swimming in the sea and of driving a car. You stay there on my lap and you dream and I will live this flatland reality for the both of us.

He locks up the TV cabinet and secures the key in the key box by the front door and locks that box with the key around his neck.

I used to think he might die.

A heart attack, cancer. Anything. A quiet death upstairs in that front bedroom; me finding him motionless and cool. Or something more dramatic. An aneurysm in his combine or a heart attack dragging coppiced wood onto the trailer behind the quad. I was sure he'd die one day. And I used to imagine heaving his dead weight up with a pulley and a rope, some kind of lift system, so I could get that neck key up to the key box to open it and reach the Land Rover key and get away from this place. He'd be too heavy, I know that. I'd use the bolt cutters he used on me. I'd snip off the thick chain from his neck and I wouldn't beat his body with the bolt cutters, I'd stop myself from going that far.

Lenn says good night and then he goes down to the half-cellar with a bucketful of overripe bananas and two bowls with dried-up custard in the bottom—I left as much as I could without him noticing anything—and he's taking bacon fat and one raw egg, out of date.

I change Huong. I still keep the spare cloths and pins and Vaseline and a bowl of clean water and some paper towels under the sofa. I can sense him down there. With her. She is still alive but they say nothing to each other. The gaps between the floorboards are big enough for me to tell. Not big enough for me to pass her anything through, not wide enough for her finger to pass between, even if I could risk that kind of thing anymore. Which I can't. I have nothing whatsoever left to be burned.

He comes up, bolts the door, looks at me.

"Jane," he says, looking me up and down. "You still leakin' from havin' the young'un?"

22

Last night we had a sharp frost. When I look out of the kitchen window this morning, the dank featureless plateau all around us is silver-white with ice crystals blasted onto every blade of grass and every stiff wave of mud. The world is still.

Huong's sleeping better these days, her stomach has enlarged—that's what I believe anyway—and she can take more formula from the bottle. I still have the same two proper baby bottles and I treat each as if it were a precious family heirloom, some rare and valuable artwork; I treasure them both the same. She's getting stronger and my fear—that stiffness in my skin from wondering how long Huong can live for, what more I can do, how I can help her—it's fading.

But he's watching me. Not to see if I'm doing my chores, he's loosened up on the tapes, but he's watching me like he used to when I arrived. When I take a bath he's there in the doorframe. Staring. Observing. When I go to the toilet, when I undress in the small back bedroom. He hasn't asked me to his room yet but it's only a matter of time.

I fill the firebox with coppiced willow and open the vents to help it take and then I go outside to bring in more wood. He does the heavy lifting, my hips and knees are too skewed now, my ankle too loose, like some overcooked mutton joint.

Scratching.

She's down there scratching at the floorboards. Like a mouse. An emaciated mouse. I can hear her blackened fingernails scraping along the underside of these boards, splinters of wood collecting underneath each nail, her tips rasping against the grain of the wood. There are no words. I have no letters and no ID card and no clothes and no passport and no book. Nothing. So if I step out of line all I have is Huong. And the two baby bottles. And the Vaseline, which is running low. I'm rationing it. If I upset him he will punish me by punishing Huong because she is the one with all the things now, not me.

I slip down to the floor, mindful of my crushed ankle, mindful not to damage it more. The skin is changing color, bruised all the time now. Loose. Numb yet still painful. I get to the floor and bring out the changing things and unpin her diaper. Soon I'll need to fold the fabric in a different way, soon she'll be too big for the way I fold it now.

There's a voice underneath me.

"Help."

I look down but I can't see through the boards. The camera's at my back. I remove the soiled cloth and fold it over on itself and clean her.

"Help me."

It's more of a wheeze than anything else. More of a cough than a voice. How cold must she be down there? How damp? How sick? I whisper "I will" to the floor, my back to the camera over by the locked TV cabinet. I whisper "Don't give up," and then I scramble to the Rayburn and stoke the flames with the poker and will it hotter, and I will the heat to travel down not up.

Huong and I take a nap and I have a heavy weight of guilt in the pit of my stomach, weighing me down into the mattress, his mother's mattress. I feed my baby and she drinks. Instead of Steinbeck, I recite passages from Kim-Ly's early letters. And I tell her of the fruits and vegetables of home. I talk her through the planets of the solar system, and the largest land animals on earth. I explain about the continents and how some of them are moving apart and some are crashing together. Mountain ranges and ocean ridges. Volcanoes. I list rivers from home, each one teeming with fish, as many as I can remember from my school days, from geography classes, and then I work through her family, our family, the tree spreading out in my mind, the names comforting to me as I share them with her, this uncle and that late great-grandmother and this cousin and all her second cousins. She is not alone.

We sleep.

Her coughing wakes me. Not a baby cough, but some kind of bark, a dry animal croak. I look at her and place my palm against her forehead. She's hot. I take her downstairs and give her some water and make her up a new bottle. Huong's crying when he walks in.

"Shut Mary up, will you? I'm as cold as a dead hare."

I offer the bottle to her and sit her in my arm but she writhes around and she's hotter now, sweating, her hair damp, curling.

"You shut it up or I will."

"She has a fever."

"Don't care what it is, I've been workin' out there all day sprayin', and last thing a man wants when he walks back indoors is all that yellin' and slobberin'."

"I'll take her back upstairs," I say.

"Didn't you hear what I said? Make me a mug of tea and shut her up."

I boil the packets of cod in parsley sauce on the hot plate. The Rayburn's about as hot as it'll go on account of me trying to warm the half-cellar, but it's making Huong worse. Whatever I do I seem to inflict harm to one of them. I'm failing both. Huong squirms in my arms and coughs and her skin is flushed red.

"Lenn, look at her."

He walks out and then walks back in with an armful of coppiced willow and drops it into the basket by the stove.

"Give her a cold bath after dinner, that'll fix it."

Maybe he's right? How do I know? This is what grandmothers and neighbors are for, and doctors, nurses, and wise local women who have seen these things a hundred times before.

She settles a little and we eat. There's scratching from immediately beneath me and I talk louder than usual to cover the sound of it. And then, when my volume is too suspicious, I pinch Huong on the fat part of her leg so she starts crying to cover up the scratching because no good can come of him getting more agitated than he already is. If I need a doctor or some medicine for her, he'll need to be kept happy.

"Why don't you run a nice hot bath and I'll take the young'un."

"She's not well, Lenn."

"Just needs her father more than likely, you run a hot bath and I'll tend to her."

I bathe as quickly as I can, my ears attuned to any noise in the main room. When I get out, a towel around my head, she's asleep in his arms.

He winks at me and I take her from him.

"Nothin' on the box tonight," he says. "Best turn in, night like this. I'll feed the pigs in the mornin'."

We go upstairs, him helping me up each step, me cradling Huong from every lurch so she can get some sleep to fight whatever sickness she has. Whatever infection or virus. She's sweating. Red. As hot as a roast chicken in my arms.

"Put her down in there, she'll be alright."

I place her down on the single bed in the back bedroom and she's wheezing in her sleep. Restless. Her tiny heart is racing. I surround her with pillows and he passes me the thin cotton sheet and the small towel and says he'll be back up in a minute.

From space right now, looking down, you'd see a small rooftop with a smoky chimney sitting at the center of a huge flat series of fields interconnected with tracks and low hedges and dikes. There might be a thin crust of ice atop the still dike waters. A glass lid. The land is white. From space right now, looking down through the layers of atmosphere, you'd see a roof and then a mother and her child, wheezing, overheating, and then a man washing himself in the bathroom he built, and then another woman barely existing underneath it all in the cold and the dark.

I pull off my nightie, his mother's nightie. I place the towel on the other side of his bed and lie down and I half cover myself with the sheet.

This is the worst.

I will him to speed up and to never, ever, ever try to give me pleasure. I implore him. It will never happen, I will not allow it, not at all. Idiot. Imposter. Base creature. He is over me, his face clear through the thin sheet, when she wakes up. I lurch upright, my weakened stomach muscles tightening, my spine responding to her gasps, and he pushes me back down softly.

She coughs but it's barking really, some sick little dog. She fights for breath and she coughs and my eyes are tears, wet on the sheet. He's still being slow. I will a heart attack on him, some vein collapsing, some arterial blockage swooping to his brain, a stroke, a catastrophic hemorrhage. But he keeps on. She sobs in the other room, twenty feet from me, alone. He moves away and I get up and throw the sheet on the floor, him behind me curled up with that towel in the fetal position, and I pick her up and hold her to my mouth and look at her and stroke her neck. She's breathing but she sounds like she's full of mucus, like something's wrong with her tubes. I rub her back and her eyes roll in their sockets. Oh, no. No, please, Huong, no. I walk around the small back bedroom and I want to slam the door shut so it's just her and me in here, but that's against his rules. I cannot do a single thing that might set him off.

I take her into the bed. I cover us both with sheets and blankets because the air up here is cold and it is heavy. I take the bottle I prepared earlier. It's lukewarm now, the temperature of the blood inside my body. I offer her the formula and she shuns it. I take her to my breast for warmth and then I give her the bottle and she drinks a little, coughing and spluttering against my skin.

He's there in the doorway.

"You get cleaned up downstairs and I'll have a good look at young'un, case she needs the doctor from down the village."

Okay. That's progress. I will do as he says if there's hope. I hand her to him, me shrouded in a sheet from the back bedroom, her shrouded in a moth-eaten blanket. I go down and wash and pray to the horizon that he might take her to a qualified doctor or buy her some baby medicine at a pharmacy in the large town past the bridge, or from the Tesco where he bought the two bottles and the formula.

I go back upstairs.

He's in the front bedroom with her, him sitting on the edge of the bed, her cradled in his arms. She looks content there.

He looks up at me.

"Don't reckon she looks like a Mary, this young'un, wrong face for a Mary, what do you reckon?" He touches the tip of her nose. "Ain't no Mary like I've seen in me life, this one. Reckon we got her name wrong with this young'un."

Huong wheezes and coughs and looks over at me, her eyes half closed.

"Reckon we'll call her Janey from now on, what do you say, eh? Looks like a little Janey, this one, reckon she's a Janey through and through."

23

I wake every hour or so through the night. Each time Huong moves or coughs or cries out I'm awake in two blinks, alert and ready for her. Despite the horse pills. I'm drugged but I think I'm alert. And now the light is returning to the fields, about an hour from proper sunrise I'd say, and I am utterly exhausted.

She's not hot. In the night she went from fever to chills, shivering, her shoulders shaking. If she had teeth they would have chattered. But now the fever seems to have passed, or gone down. I wish we had a thermometer in the house, some means by which I could judge her health. I've asked but he's never brought one home. I don't know her weight or her height or her blood type. I feel it all, I know it inside of myself, but the numbers would be reassuring. Like a passport or birth certificate. And I yearn for her being seen by my parents. For my mother to rock her in her arms and my father to place his finger in her tiny palm. It'd make it all more permanent, more safe.

He's up early to feed the pigs and by the time he gets back we're downstairs and she's asleep in double blankets on the sofa, still wheezing. Has the damp from this place caught in her chest? Is this tuberculosis? Something else that all other babies these days are vaccinated against?

"Ain't a whole bowlful left in the package," he says, shaking the box of cornflakes.

I shrug. Tired. Defeated.

"Don't reckon there is. Most of it's dust. I'll take it down."

He unbolts the door to the half-cellar. No voices, no scratches. A chill sour wind rises up and sweeps around the walls and Huong coughs on the plastic-wrapped sofa and a line of saliva joins her lips to the plastic. The stove chimney roars in the wall. He comes straight back up and bolts the door. Must have left the cornflakes box on the ladder.

"I'm used to the name Mary," I say. "I've been calling her Mary for months now, she's our Mary."

Please. Please never call her the other name again. That is not her. Do not continue this hideous purgatory. It ends with me.

He shakes his head.

"She's Janey now, best get used to it. She looks like a Jane to me. She's a Janey, that young'un, just have to look at her to know it."

I grip the steel rail of the Rayburn stove to keep my composure. I squeeze it in my palms until my knuckles feel tight in their sockets. She is no such thing.

"Maybe I'll go down to the village later, maybe Spar or even the big'un up past the bridge. Janey got much food left, has she?"

"One tub left."

"Alright then."

He leaves and I take Huong down to the floor. She's so unspeakably pale. More pale than I have ever seen her. Chalk-white. I unpin her diaper. Something's stuck so I fiddle with the blunt safety pin, his mother's, and then the diaper stains red and it's her blood on my fingers. I turn her gently and I see the pinprick. I did this? I pinned her own diaper *through* her skin? How? When? Last night? She didn't scream when I pinned her? I dab the blood with the old diaper cloth. Must have been just before sunrise. Her last change. Or the waking before that, pitch-black, the dead of night. How alert am I in the darkness? With these pills in my system? How many times did I change her last night? I wounded my own sick child and she didn't have the energy to cry out.

I bring her to my face and touch my cheek to hers and she is too cold. I scoot on my backside to the Rayburn and I can't lean against it, it's too hot, but I sit close to it, my back against the rear of his armchair. She didn't cry out? With a pin stuck through her?

Scratching noises.

I move my bad leg, my mangled ankle, and slip down until I'm lying on the floorboards. I turn my face to the heat.

More scratching, directly beneath me.

"Cynth?" I whisper.

She's starts to cry down there.

"You know my name," she says.

I start to cry as well, my tears falling to the dry wood I scrubbed yesterday.

"I can't pass you things, he's closed the hole."

"I know," she says. "I want nothing. Just waiting. Not long now."

"No," I say, Huong warming up in my arms, wheezing, her heart racing. "You must stay with me."

"I'm not with you," she says. "I am not with anyone. I am underneath you all."

And then my eyes widen and I look up to the light of the window.

"Cynth," I say. "You there?"

"Yes."

"Let's leave, the three of us. Let's make it out."

"I can't," she says. "I'm too weak."

"My baby," I say, my head turned to her, the floorboards in between our lips, my tears falling to the wood fibers and dust. "She's getting sick. And he has plans for her. He's getting desperate, I can feel it. He knows they're out there searching for you. He's like a rat backed into a corner. We can't wait, Cynth, I cannot let you stay down there any longer. There is no option."

"No," she says. "You go. I'm too weak. You don't know."

I turn my face and Huong is looking at me with great intensity, her eyes large and clear now. And there are birds at the window, birds lined up on the telegraph pole outside, a dozen or more crows. One flies away. They all fly away.

"Next time he goes to town," I say. "The three of us. You and I can support each other and we'll need to move fast. I know the way. We can get out together."

"Leave me here," she says.

"You do not understand," I say. "I can't leave without you, I cannot walk. And my baby cannot leave without me. If you stay we all stay."

There's a spit in the firebox and the chimney roars up by the roof.

Huong and I both look down at the floor, waiting.

"I'll try," she says.

Lenn comes back for his sandwich. Get out of this godforsaken cottage you demon. Leave us.

"Dead eel near the dike up by the pigs, saw it comin' back here, stiff as a pipe."

Leave us.

"Gonna stick it in the nettle patch. Ain't a snake, just a fat eel. Leave it be. And anyone comes around here, you get yourself upstairs and don't make a whisper. I got Frank Trussock keepin' an eye out, I ain't stupid. Any bother and I'll put you out with the pigs for a night or two, see how you like it out there by the marshes."

I nod.

"How's Janey feeling? You lookin' after her proper?"

"She's sick," I say, my back rigid. "Please buy medicine. Infant acetaminophen. To reduce the fever."

He sticks out his bottom lip and looks at her and takes his coat and takes the keys to his Land Rover from the locked key box by the front door.

"Have me pie ready at five," he says.

Go.

I watch his Land Rover drive away, the red lights at the back shrinking, morphing into the pinpricks of blood I left on Huong's hip earlier today.

The bolts.

I look at the top bolt and then look back through the front door. I touch it and then pull back. What if he forgot something? What if he comes back? I touch the bolt again and Huong is asleep in my arms, pale, clammy. I pull on the end of the bolt. I swallow and then I push it hard. The door loosens in its frame. I look back and he is not there. The two bottles are full and hot, ready to go. I've had an extra half horse pill to help with the pain. He's not coming back, the track is clear. I move the lower bolt. It's stuck firm. I look back. Nothing. It's safe. The coast is clear. Huong wheezes in my arms and I move my foot and my size eleven sandal strap, his sandal strap, catches on the doorframe to the main room and pulls my bad foot the wrong way and my face twists and contorts with pain.

I bite down on my tongue, the sharp front teeth bearing down, then there's blood in my mouth. Something else to feel. I pull the lower bolt and the door swings open and the cold, damp air hits me and it hits Huong. Smells like old garbage down there. Rotten meat.

"Cynth?" I shout. "Are you coming? He's gone."

There is nothing. Nobody.

"Cynth, please. Hurry up, he's gone to town, we don't have long."

Nothing. Nobody.

But I cannot climb down this steep wooden ladder into the half-cellar. I'd never make it back up again.

"Cynth!" I scream.

Something moves. I see a shadow down on the floor. But, no, it's not a shadow, it is her. Crawling. She's blackened and her eyes are red.

"Come up," I yell, Huong hot in my arms, the sweat from her head soaking into my sleeve. "Hurry."

She creeps to the lower rung and climbs up. With each step toward ground level she grows more wretched. When she's at the top I hold Huong and I try to help her get to her feet. She is arched like a hunchback, her head down by her chest. She's wearing the horsey jodhpurs but they are not beige like last time I saw them, they are brown now. Dark brown. Her red hair is black with sludge and it is matted. Her skin is both translucent and filthy at the same time.

"We have to go," I say.

"Where is he?" she says, her voice trembling.

"Gone to town," I say.

She crosses herself.

"But he'll be back soon. We need to start walking."

She steps outside. Her frame is diminished by half. She's a starving bird, the clothes hanging from her bones. She smells so strongly it makes my eyelids squeeze together. And yet I owe her everything.

"I need food," she says.

"Later," I say.

"The milk," she says.

I have two bottles of formula in my apron pocket. They're for Huong, nobody else. But reluctantly I offer her one and she unscrews the lid and drinks half of it and then she throws it straight up.

"No!" I say. "Not so fast."

She sips from the bottle and screws on the nipple and we set off toward the road. There are roads in the distance, to the left of us and to the right, but they're too far away. We must walk up the track and get past the locked halfway gate.

She looks at my ankle and pulls my arm around her neck. We hobble together, my twisted right ankle flopping around, Huong wrapped in all the blankets, tight under my arm.

"God bless you both," says Cynth. "You saved me."

I say nothing. We get a decent pace up, me leaning on her, it works quite well. She's weak, I can feel the sharpness of her shoulder digging into my armpit, but she doesn't complain.

The air is cold and crisp.

"My house is twelve miles from here," she says, gasping, spitting on the ground. "All this time, my house is just over there." She looks into the distance. "I can almost see it."

"What's that?" I say.

There are lights ahead, tiny white pinpricks.

"It's a car, it could be help," says Cynth.

"It's him," I say, turning us around. "Quick. We have to go. Run."

We hobble faster, no need to conserve energy. We run. We make it back to the cottage and I push her inside and look back and he's there at the locked halfway gate. Did he see us? From back there could he see her with me?

I push her toward the half-cellar door.

"No," she pleads, her hands fixed on the frame. "Let me talk to him."

"We'll try again tomorrow," I say.

"No," she says. "I can't go back down there."

I look back through the front door window and he's there, he's twenty feet away. I push her but she's so weak she offers no resistance. I close the door and bolt the top and she sobs on the other side and then I bolt the bottom and he walks inside.

24

Can he sense how fast my heart is beating, how hard it's banging against my ribs? Does he know that we left this place?

I'm behind schedule for his dinner because I didn't expect to ever be cooking it. Chicken pie. I make a hash of it, some ugly pie-like thing in his mother's pie tin and throw it in the Rayburn and fill the firebox with willow and open the vents and urge the thing to cook.

He comes back inside and takes off his coat. It's too desperate, how close we were, how cruel things have turned out with her back down there and me and Huong still up here and me boiling potatoes for him in his mother's skillet on the hot plate.

"Smellin' alright, that is," he says, sniffing the air. "I'll scrub up."

He goes into the bathroom.

Not the tapes, do not look at the tapes. Do not. Please do anything but that.

"I'll just look at them tapes."

He sits down and switches on the computer. It whirs and beeps. The screen flashes. So, this is it? How will he do it? In what order?

I take Huong into my arms from the plastic-wrapped sofa and

she looks scared like she knows exactly what's about to happen. Her lips are pursed. She's hot and red and her eyes are twitching, not focusing on my face, looking around the room.

Poker? Knife? I've thought these thoughts a hundred times before. A thousand. I cannot fight him; he's too strong, too heavy. It's as pointless as fighting a tidal wave or a cliff. The computer screen fills with me. And Huong. On the toilet, in the bed, making his tea in his pesticide mug. I step over to the kitchen sink. "There's a wasp," I say. There is no wasp. I push on the window but leave the lower latch locked. I push and then ball a fist and I thump through the lower left pane of glass as if it were his forehead.

The sound of glass breaking startles Huong.

"What in the hell?" he says, standing up. There are glass shards all over my hand, blood trickling into the white enamel sink, the sink I have scrubbed white every day for the past seven years. "What you doin', you daft woman?"

Huong has tiny shards of glass on her face. Triangles. Some equilateral, others isosceles, I remember the shapes from school. I look at her perfect skin and her eyes and I can remember the interior angles. The tapes are playing on the computer and as he stands out in the garden knocking out the remaining glass, the fragments clinging to the putty surrounding the pane, I watch on the screen as Cynth and Huong and I leave this house. Lenn taps out the glass pieces with his sleeve covering his hand. He says, "I'd better get me tools from the shed, board it up right, you can get on with cleanin' up that mess on the floor and don't go spoilin' me pie neither."

A stay of execution.

He walks away and I stand in between him and the computer. When he's gone I turn and watch the empty main room and hear him open up his shed. I look at the screen and see myself push Cynth down into the half-cellar and see him come back. I let it run on. The pie smells like it's almost ready in the stove.

After dinner we sit watching TV with the Rayburn door open, a square piece of plywood screwed over the window hole. The room lost a few degrees of heat in the time it took Lenn to board over the missing pane and it's struggling to regain them.

"Did you cancel your shopping trip?" I ask, his hand on my head. He is at his most calm during this farce, this charade of a happy family evening, me on the floor, him in his chair, the remote balancing on his armrest.

"Yeah," he says.

I sit and rock Huong to settle her and I say nothing. I know he was testing me with that quick return, that aborted shopping trip, keeping me on my toes, no privacy and no certainty, nothing of my own.

"I'll go tomorrow," he says, his fingers sliding through my hair, over my scalp like five sick snakes slithering through long grass. "I'll get young Janey some pills, some more food powder, don't fret, woman."

His fingers move sideways and my hairs pull in their follicles, my scalp stretching up to meet his hands. It's uncomfortable. I say nothing, just sit there trying to keep my daughter quiet with this man, this stranger to me, twisting his fingertips into my hair.

He feeds the pigs. Huong and I go to bed in the small back bedroom and I worry about Cynth plunged back into freezing blackness down there, bent double once again, the sweetness grasped away from her after she'd only just reached out for it.

Huong coughs and wheezes. She has a bad night. I feed her and rock her and soothe her and tell her that one day she'll be in a circle, a circle of family members and friends and neighbors, and she will not be coughing. She will not be cold or scared or hungry and she will not need to look out for her mother because I will be fine.

The next morning he takes his tools to coppice more willow.

It's a bright day: chemtrails clear in the blue sky like God's own tic-tac-toe. I feed Huong and I feed myself. She's still hot. Still less responsive than usual. With the camera watching me from the corner I heat sugar in his mother's saucepan with some water and then I pour it into a clean bottle and I walk over to Huong on the sofa. With my back to the camera I tap the floor and pick up my child. There's scratching underneath me. Weak scratching. I find the gap between the floorboards, a split as wide as a piece of paper, maybe a sheet of cardboard, and pretend to feed Huong and then the nipple falls off the bottle and the warm sugar water pours down onto the floorboards. Some drains through the gap. Most of it pools on the wood and I have to help it down with my hand.

"Silly me," I say, as if to Huong. "Clumsy me."

It's getting down to her, I think. A bottleful of sugar water. Might make her sick. Might not get to her at all. There's no noise from down there, nothing. No slurping or smacking of lips, no scratching. The sweet liquid's all gone. It's all down there.

"God bless you," she says. "I'm ready now."

"Wait," I say.

When Lenn returns I give him his presliced cheese and presliced ham sandwich and a bag of salted chips.

"I'm off to shop in a bit, but if the traffic is busy and snarled up near the bridge I'll come straight back here and do it tomorrow."

He looks at me.

"Okay," I say. Must not urge him, must not.

I have two full bottles ready, hot ones. The blankets are tucked under the sofa. I have the remnants of my sandwiches, not so much that he'd notice, not so little that it wouldn't help Cynth. These are sugared too. She'll need a boost to her energy if we're to get all the way to the road and this is the best way I can think of.

He puts on his coat.

He pulls on one of his boots. Then the other.

"What's that pill you talked about, the one for little Jane? For her hotness?"

"Acetaminophen," I say.

"We'll see," he says, and then he unlocks the key box and takes his Land Rover key and locks up the key box and walks out the door.

My heart is pounding and so is Huong's. It's as if she knows. Or else it's her sickness intensifying. We stand at the Rayburn. Her body is too limp. She's cold now and I want her as warm as possible before we do this, as full as possible. Lenn gets to the locked halfway gate. My ears are ringing at the thought of what we will do. I see him start the engine, gray smoke pumping out of the back of it and freezing into low puffs of fog near the ground. He puts his lights on. He drives off up the track.

I hobble through to the half-cellar door as fast as I can and unbolt it and she's right there waiting this time, her eyes glowing in the murk.

"Thank you," she says.

"Hold her for a second," I say, passing Huong to her. It feels wrong giving her away. Huong screams and scratches out with her hands. I take the blankets and shove both bottles down into my apron.

Cynth has more red on her cheeks now and she's wiped herself with something, some water or spittle; she looks cleaner this time. She takes Huong to the Rayburn and speaks to her and strikes a match against the Swan Vestas box—it's almost empty now—and tries to calm her with the bright flame but my daughter will not be calmed.

I take Huong and we step outside into the cold November air.

"No," says Cynth, pointing up the track toward the locked half-way gate. "This won't work."

I tug Cynth's sleeve.

"We have to go," I say. "I don't know how long he'll be, we have to leave now."

She shakes me off and walks with her back bent over, around the corner of the house. Filthy. She scans the horizon while I follow her, rocking Huong in my arms.

"We have to go . . ."

"There's a small road that way," she says, interrupting me, pointing in the opposite direction of the track and the locked halfway gate. "Less traffic but we'll have a better chance."

I hobble to her. I look into the nothingness which is that direction. The vastness. The uninterrupted distance. Hope is the other way: food and the Spar shop and the village and every car I've ever seen here comes from this other way. I've dreamed of escaping in this direction. It's the way out.

"It's too far," I say. "Cynth, the road that way is too far, the trucks are smaller than on the main road, I can't make it."

She looks back to the locked halfway gate and the yard. She looks at my ankle.

"If we leave up that track he'll intercept us," she says. "Or he'll find us on the road when he gets back. We should walk back there, to that pig barn. That's about halfway, that's our resting stop. If he comes back from the shops and we've made it out that far then we've still got a chance. He won't know we're there, he won't expect it. He'll go up the track as normal looking for us."

She's shivering as she tells me this. Her cheeks are curved inward and her red hair, her matted red hair, is shiny with grease in the clear light.

"If we make it that far and he comes home," she says, "then maybe you and her can hide and I can run for it, run to that side road and get help, flag down a car. Call the police. He'll think we went the other way. This is our best chance."

I look toward hope, toward the road I arrived on, and then I look at the endless flatlands she's gazing at. She sees hope there. I see endless fields he's planted, he's tended, sloping down toward the sea, nothing good in that direction, the only thing that comes from that way is weather.

"You're sure?" I say.

She nods and puts her arm around me for support and I take the weight off my bent ankle.

"Let's go," she says.

We walk along the gravel and try to avoid making footprints. We pass the dead eel, rotting, its skeleton like some prehistoric fossil, and we pass the ash pile, the resting place of my belongings, and then we skirt the edge of the closest field. It's stubble now, tiny remnants of wheat, and they crunch under my size eleven sandals. We've been walking for ten minutes and my feet are already frozen but it helps with the pain, it numbs me. Each footfall feels like stepping on upturned drinking straws, the ones we use for soft drinks back home. Cynth's shoulder pokes into my armpit and we stagger and try to keep rhythm, try to keep going. Huong's not making a sound. She either understands what we're doing or else she's even more sick than I feared.

At the end of the first field we cross a small ditch and step over a stile and the next field is larger. Plowed. The ridges are frozen and sparkling, each piece of dirt fixed in time and space, the surface so uneven we almost fall every few paces. We stay to the edge of the field but he's plowed close to the ditch.

Her wrists are covered in scratches or cuts.

I look back at the farm cottage. I've never seen it from this distance, from this angle. The bathroom extension looks like my ankle: substandard, the wrong angle, affixed crudely onto one side.

"Keep going," says Cynth. "Keep it up. You're doing really well."

But it is she who is doing well. She is a buckled skeleton haunting these November fields, her eyes red from the light, her bent frame so slight beside mine.

I give her a candy from my pocket, one of the three I removed from the walls this morning. She grabs it from me and I hear it rattle around her yellow teeth and we seem to walk faster for a while.

A pair of pheasants, a cock and a hen, a couple, fly out of a low hedge and land halfway up the field. Toward the cottage, toward the willow smoke from the Rayburn stove. They're going the wrong way.

Huong moves inside my coat, his mother's coat. And then she screams. I stop and Cynth stops and I try to comfort her, rock her, speak to her. I tell her we're doing okay, and tell her to stay strong. But she wails and then she starts to bark again. Wheezing. I pull the bottle from my pocket, lukewarm now, and give her a one-minute feed, Cynth looking anxious in my peripheral vision, scanning the horizon, keeping watch, staring at the track and the locked halfway gate. I withdraw the nipple and Huong grasps for it and I tell her "later, more later," and she screams all the more loudly. I push her into my chest and shush her and we set off.

"Is it too far?" I say, more to myself than to Cynth.

"No, we're almost halfway to the pig barn," she says. "The worst part is over. Let's keep up this rhythm."

My breath is making clouds in the air. We pass through into another field, grain sprinkled on the earth. Weeds lie withered in the tractor tire grooves which tessellate each field with shallow tracks. There's a patch of wetland we try to skirt but my sandals get muddy and suddenly each step is a trial. I scrape my sandal on the ground but the mud is glue and my good foot weighs almost as much as my bad one.

George and Lennie and a mouse. Thanh and Cynth and a two-month-old angel.

There's an elevation in this field, maybe three feet above the general flatland level, perhaps six feet above sea level. When we crest it and cross a hedge, we see the dike. Cynth says nothing and I say nothing and we just keep walking. But we're both looking up and down its length, looking for a crossing point, a bridge or a narrowing. And there are none. None to help us anyway. The two I can see are miles away, maybe four miles away in either direction.

"How are we . . . ?"

"We just will," she says.

"Can you swim?" I say.

"Can you?" she says. "It won't be deep. We'll wade through."

I look back and the cottage is tiny now, light gray smoke billowing from the chimney, rising vertically for a while and then diagonally, up to the clouds and the huge open skies. It's too far to go back. We have reached that point, my sandals caked with heavy mud, Huong furious at my chest, where we are stranded in between two hells.

"Can we stop for five minutes?" I ask. "She needs a feed. I have a sandwich for you."

Cynth is panting. I have no idea how she goes on, how she finds the reserves to do this after her months bent double underground. Her elbows are sharp as razors and I can see bare patches of scalp where her red hair has either fallen out or else been pulled out in clumps.

"We'll stop at the barn," she says. "If we stop now we won't make it, we'll stop when we get to the pig barn. Give me the sandwich. You try to feed her as we walk."

I hand her the presliced cheese and presliced ham sandwich and I take a candy for myself and I try to feed Huong. It's a struggle. With every hobble we take, a farce of a pathetic three-legged race with no other competitors, completed on the surface of some hostile planet, the bottle slips from her mouth or I almost fall. Her nose is running constantly and her breaths are turning shallow. My bad ankle is muddied and the bones inside are scraping together. I have no more horse pills. None.

I'm preparing myself for the water. The ice? How do you cross a dike with a baby and a twisted, mangled ankle, in November, in men's size eleven sandals? How?

But Huong manages the whole bottle and then she falls asleep, the rocking of our endless footsteps and missteps sending her off into a peaceful doze, a sleep of freedom and hope and family and joy. Dreams. But it could be too deep a sleep. It could be. I have an urge to wake her. To check her. Cynth has finished her sandwich and we're walking faster now, getting closer to the barn, the width of the dike seeming to grow with every footstep. A hare bursts from the low hedgerow and sprints across this rough field like it could go three times as fast if it chose to. What does this look like? The three of us dragging ourselves, one another, through the mud, skirting the edges of these vast featureless fields, his fields, and that hare just deciding to leave and then leaving. How does that look?

Cynth stumbles on a ridge of stiff earth and brings me down with her. I see the barn twist as I fall. Our legs get tangled and I land hard on my right ankle and nothing cracks, but the joint bends under me like chilled pork jelly. When I straighten up, the shards of bone in the joint, if you can even call it that, scrape one another, and pain flares up and I throw my head back. Squinting, grimacing, I feel Huong wake up. The agony. I cannot go on. I am broken.

"I'm sorry," says Cynth. "It's my fault, I'm so sorry."

I can't talk right now. I focus everything on not blacking out, on gritting myself to keep conscious. My teeth are clenched, my nostrils flared, I have no tears to offer this fresh agony.

A plane passes overhead. I look up and watch it pass silently through a small cloud and out the other side. Calm and steady. Full of people going about their normal lives. I must remember that: there are people up there in that plane going from one place to another, hundreds of people most likely, and I could be one of them one day.

We trudge on.

The barn is still miles in the distance; the landscape's tricking us, the flatness of the fields a curse, an illusion, a cruel game. But we're coming up to the dike. The waters are still. It's medium size I'd say, fifteen feet across, maybe twelve.

I see the clouds reflected in the unmoving dike water and look down at my wet, mud-encrusted sandals and I pray to the horizon to get us safely across this thing.

Cynth helps me down the bank.

The grass on either side of the silver-black water is dead. Bile-yellow. We scramble down to the water's edge, me on my backside for the final few feet. I'm gripping Huong so tight she yells and I bring her up to my face, the water just inches from my muddy sandals, and kiss her.

"We're leaving that place," I say to her. "We're leaving, my love, and I will take care of us both."

Cynth pokes a dead piece of wheat into the water to test the depth but it's too flaccid and just floats on the top. She peers down.

"Not deep," she says, sweeping her filthy hair from her face, her fingers leaving marks in the grime by her ears. She turns to me. "Not too deep, I don't think."

I look along the dike. It is as straight as the magnetic strip on the back of a credit card. And as shiny. It ends at the bridge which is now our horizon, but I know it ends many, many miles away from here, toward the sea.

"If I fall . . . ," I say.

"You won't fall," says Cynth.

I dip my hand into the water and move it around and the reflected sky distorts and twists and sinks to the bottom.

The water is ice-cold. It's so still it looks like liquid metal rather than water. There are no insects buzzing around its surface like there are in summertime. No living things at all.

We step in.

Arm in arm, hesitantly, we nudge into the freezing water.

The bottom is close but it is soft. It tricks us. I take a step and lose my size eleven sandal and turn and fall into the water, my arms up over my head, Huong squirming with me underneath her.

"Take her," I say, gasping, thrashing around, spitting dirty water from my mouth.

Cynth pulls me up and takes Huong and she screams.

"I can't find it, it's gone," I say.

"Your sandal?"

"It's gone," I say, gasping for air, my teeth chattering.

Cynth gives Huong back to me and I stand there with my bad foot resting on the silt, the weight on it excruciating, my molars grinding into each other.

She feels around for it, shivering like some abominable bog creature.

She shakes her head.

We wade together, her helping my weight, Huong tight in my arm, and we move across the low, stinking dike, the water almost up to our armpits.

It's so unspeakably cold.

"Just keep going," says Cynth. "We're doing well."

I look at her and focus on not losing my footing. She's still shivering. Her red hair is wet and the strands have moved to reveal more bald patches. Poor Cynth. My sock is full of mud. I'm in up to my waist now, damp to my chest. Ice-cold. Huong is shivering but I pull her tight to me and I breathe on the back of her neck to warm her. We splash out the other side, me with one sandal, Cynth with weeds in her hair, and sit on the bank.

"Eels," says Cynth, panting for breath, shuddering, wringing out her trousers and fleece. "Did you feel them?"

I shake my head. What godforsaken pit is this flatland place? Why was it ever reclaimed from the seas?

She helps me up the slope and I help her. It's steeper on this side, higher. And then we peek back toward the cottage like a soldier might have once peeked out of a trench or foxhole. Nothing. The smoke is rising from the chimney and the Land Rover is not at the locked halfway gate. Lenn's still out.

"Half an hour more," says Cynth. "Then we're at the barn, somewhere to stop, you can feed her maybe, quickly, then we're off to the road. We're getting there." She crosses herself.

We set off but I cannot stop shivering. I'm getting forgetful. Tired. The wind freezes my wet apron to my legs and Huong is as heavy as a six-year-old. Cynth is driven by some invisible power, some force, pushing her, pulling her, helping her. Or maybe it's just the things she's seen in that half-cellar, the pitiful kindnesses she heard afforded to me that she never received.

This field is stony. I feel every step on the underside of my unclad foot, like some animal forced to walk on rough ground. Each flint shard, each hardened lump of earth digs into me, into my one good foot, the one leg I rely on to carry me and my daughter away from this fenland existence.

But we are making progress. The barn is growing on the horizon and now I can see the trucks on the small road Cynth talked about, the white trucks at least, and the tractors. I haven't seen a bus yet, but I'd take help from a bicycle on this day, from a pedestrian.

Huong shivers.

She shivers against my chest and her face is turning blue. Did she get wet from the dike? Or is it her heavy cloth diaper, the fluid against her perfect skin freezing her minute by minute? I breathe onto her. I urge the heat out of myself and into her skin, into her blood. Want that transfer to be fast. My heat to her. When we cross the next stile I reach down for her bottle, her formula, and it is cold to the touch. How can I save her from this wind?

We climb over the stile and Cynth pulls away and I pull her back. "Wait," I say. "She's too cold."

Cynth looks at me and then down to Huong and I see the alarm in her reddened eyes. She comes to me and opens her jacket and pushes herself into me and we shelter Huong from the flatland winds like two sides of an oyster shell protecting a pearl. She blows on Huong's face and I blow on her neck and I rub her back and then Cynth slides her hands together very fast and then rubs Huong's legs inside her blankets. I can feel new warmth. From nothing more than two women willing it to happen: two women, strangers, friends, forcing their own warmth together to make a family of sorts out here.

Huong is contented. She is calmer and Cynth looks less concerned, so we set off toward the pig barn, glancing over our shoulders every few strides toward the cottage and the track. The chimney smoke is faint now. He's not back. But he will be.

My good foot gets stuck in mud and my bad foot feels like nothing.

We skirt the edge of an oilseed rape field. It was boldest yellow when Huong was born. Cynth is weakening now. It's as if the heat she gifted my daughter was her last. She offered it up without thinking and now it is Huong's and Cynth is too cold to go on.

But we do go on. There are rock fragments in the earth and my good foot can't take much more so I pause and decide to take the sandal from my right foot and move it over. Cynth helps me. She unbuckles the sandal and I bite down onto my hand. I bite deep. She pulls off the sandal and I scratch my forehead with my nails and the feeling is back at that ankle; it is unwelcome and it is back. She tries to put my good foot, a ball of dark mud and unrealized wheat seeds, into the leather straps but it does not work. All for nothing. She puts it back onto my misshapen foot and gently tightens the buckle and the pain is such that I lose my sight for a moment.

The barn's right there. Cinder-block walls, a corrugated-iron roof, some loose feed sacks and rubbish strewn about the place. It's smaller than I expected. This will be the first new building I've touched in seven years. The first Huong will ever touch. I look back at the cottage, at the stove where each of my possessions was burned one by one.

"Let's get inside," says Cynth. "You feed her quickly out of the wind and I'll keep watch. We don't have long. Then we make for the road with the barn in between us and the cottage; we'll try to use the barn as our cover."

I nod. We keep on walking. These fields are too vast, too inhuman, they are unending tests for the three of us, hellish forevers which we must keep on wading through.

We walk over discarded pig feed sacks and get to the wall of the barn, the solid cinder-block wall facing the cottage. We disconnect and I use the solid structure for support. There is no door on this side, no way in. I hold Huong and whisper to her, "Soon, my love. I'll have food for you, soon." I think of warming the bottle in my armpit or rubbing it with my hands to get some heat into the fluid but I'll probably just feed her as it is. She's hungry, she needs the comfort, the quiet ritual away from the weather, a roof over us both, me looking down at her sucking and sucking, her hand on my wrist.

There's a rusting pigpen railing on the side of the barn, some kind of outdoor area. We walk past it and the barn smells strongly of animal. We get to the edge of the wall and look inside and there are no pigs here.

There are none.

27

Cynth rests against a stack of pallets, her boots encased in dirt, and rivulets of sweat have carved paths through the grime on her face so that she looks almost engraved that way.

I check the cottage.

He's not home yet.

I go inside the barn, Huong's bottle under my armpit. She's agitated, tied to my body with a blanket, another shrouded around her, all inside my coat, his mother's coat.

It stinks of pigs in here; feces and blood.

The first half of the building is empty pig stalls, metal fencing separating each pen. Straw on the ground. Stainless-steel feeding troughs empty of all but black-and-white bird droppings, piglet feeders complete with teats pointing downward with no piglets to find them.

The bottle's getting warmer now. It's not at body temperature, but it's not chilled anymore. Cynth walks around the cinder-block partition wall and I check the cottage again.

He is not home. Yet.

"Jane," she says.

I feel even less like Jane out here, away from the cottage, away from the small back bedroom and the Rayburn and the locked TV cabinet and his mother's cloths.

I walk around to join her and the wind whistles through the gaps where the cinder-block walls meet the corrugated iron roof.

"Feed her in there if it's open. You'll get more shelter."

We step toward a camper.

It is decrepit. Could it be the thing he used to holiday in with his mother? In Skegness? It's still here? Most of the windows are boarded over or taped, and its base is propped up on loose cinder blocks.

"Get your baby out of the cold," says Cynth. "Out of the wind. I'll keep watch."

But I'm not sure I want to go inside this camper. His and his mother's. I walk to it, the gusts howling now through the corrugated-iron roof, sporadic cars in the far distance, a few hours' walk farther away from the cottage, and this does not feel like a safe place. Rustler, it says on the side. And now I can see clearly that it's locked up. There's a chain securing it to the concrete barn floor.

"All clear," says Cynth. "Get in, we'll set off again in five."

"Come inside with me," I say.

"Someone needs to keep watch," she says. "I'll get you settled and then I'll wait for you out there, alright?"

"I think it's locked."

We move in closer.

There is a small hole in the bottom right-hand corner of the camper door, a triangular cutout. The chain connected to the concrete floor of this pig barn with no pigs passes through the hole.

We look at each other and I move Huong up to the crook of my neck.

It's silent. Still. Nothing here.

"Get her fed," says Cynth. "As quick as you can. We have to move soon. He'll be back."

I reach for the fiberglass door and pull down the handle. It's unlocked. Warm musty air moves onto my face.

"Hello," says Cynth. "Anyone in here?"

Nothing.

I step up into the doorframe and the camper moves a little on its cinder-block foundations. Inside it's abandoned. Derelict. To my right is a small kitchen area, cracked plastic sink, window covered in bubble wrap. There's an Argos catalog open by the sink. Page 217. Electric lawn mowers.

"Nobody here," says Cynth.

She switches on the stove and it lights up and we look at each other.

I turn it off.

"We have to be quick," I say. "I'm okay. Keep watch. Five minutes. Three if she drinks fast."

Cynth leaves.

The bedroom area is two single beds separated by a narrow aisle, piles of rags and sheets and dirty blankets heaped on top of each one. I open the shower-room door. It's moldy but it's clean. There is toothpaste. An old variety I've never seen before.

"Come on, little one," I say, sitting down on one of the beds. I pull out the bottle from under my arm. I lift it to her mouth and she takes it like she hasn't been fed for days. She suckles and holds one cold hand to the bottle, the other to my chest, her anchor, her warmth. And then the blankets on the other bed start to move.

I stand up and back away and Huong loses her suction on the bottle and she yells, and I hobble to the doorframe. The chain that threads through the door, the one from outside, is secured to the bed. The moving bed.

I'll hide. Run.

I scoot along toward the area where the camper is secured to the concrete floor.

"Hello."

I stop.

I turn around and there is a woman standing in the fiberglass doorframe of Lenn's camper. I squint, but I already know that voice. I almost drop my own daughter. Am I dreaming? Are the horse pills making me see this? Am I dead?

"You came," she says.

28

I am colder than before, cold to my bones, and Huong is quiet.

She is standing there, her arms outstretched, the chain secured to her ankle with some kind of horrific manacle, tears rolling down her cheeks.

"No," I said. "No. It cannot be. Not you."

"You came," she says. "I knew you'd find me."

I look back but Cynth is nowhere to be seen.

"How are you here?" I say, tapping my head with my fingers. "It can't be."

I walk to her. She moves off her step and looks down at my ankle and gasps and covers her mouth with her hands.

"Thanh?" she says.

"Kim-Ly."

She's wearing layers and layers of rags and blankets, her hair long down to her hips, her body wasted away to just a frame.

I reach out my hand.

She takes it and puts it to her hollow cheek and I collapse. My brow is furrowed with a hundred urgent questions. She falls into me, Huong between us. We fuse together into an embrace so fierce that nothing, nothing whatsoever could ever break it. My palm is pushed into her cheek, my nose in her hair, her hand at the back of my head, her face nestled into my neck, close to her baby niece.

"You came," she says again, sobbing. "Oh, thank God you came."

I shake my head. "I've always been here." I point to the wall of the barn, in the direction of his cottage. "In the cottage over there. Leonard's cottage."

"You knew I was here? He chained you up as well?" She looks down at my injured ankle.

"I never knew, Kim-Ly, I never ever knew. That bastard. He told me you were deported five years ago, deported from Manchester."

Her tears flow and flow but mine are dry.

"What has he done to you?" I say, looking back at the camper, at the chain. "What has he done?"

"He wanted me here," she says. "He comes in the evenings on his quad bike. He said I was better off here than home in Vietnam. I'd have no rent, flowing clean water, electricity in the camper. I had a portable TV for three years until it broke down." She looks into my eyes and I see my mother in her, our mother. "He said you were working on a farm, a chicken farm inland. He said you were making good money, paying off your debt." She pauses. "You weren't?"

I shake my head.

"I was here," I say. "And you were here?"

She looks down at Huong.

"Is she yours?"

"She is."

Kim-Ly smiles. And then her smile sours.

"And his?"

"No," I say. "She is mine."

She nods and we let our foreheads meet with a bump, we kiss each other's cheeks, we hold on to each other and let the rest of the world spin around us.

"No sign," shouts Cynth, coming around the boundary wall. "Oh, sweet Jesus, who are you?"

Kim-Ly's eyes are wide open, looking at Cynth, looking at me, panicked.

"She's a friend, Kim-Ly," I say. "Cynth is a friend. She's helping me."

"Do you know each other?" asks Cynth, walking to us, eyeing up the chain bolted to the ground, the other end tight around Kim-Ly's ankle.

"This . . . ," I say, and then my tears come. I touch her hair. "This is my sister. My baby sister."

"He did this to you?" asks Cynth, pointing at the chain.

Kim-Ly nods.

"We have to go," says Cynth. "We mustn't wait any longer. We have to move right now. He's on his way back."

"We can't," I say.

"He'll be back soon," says Cynth, her eyes ablaze. "You know he will. Look what he does to people," she screams. "Look." She points to Kim-Ly's ankle.

"I'll feed Huong first," I say. "Then we'll all go together."

My sister looks at me and looks at Cynth and then she holds up the chain attached to her ankle.

"Please," she says to both of us, her chain in her hand. "Take me with you."

29

Cynth takes a loose cinder block and cracks the chain close to where it disappears into the concrete floor. The block chips and Cynth squints as the fragments fly up toward her eyes. The thick metal loops clang and chime with each impact and then the cinder block splits into two pieces.

"I have tried it," says Kim-Ly. "I've tried everything possible."

"I'll look for something," says Cynth.

I watch her run out of the barn and look back over the flat fields toward the cottage and the half-cellar below. She looks back at me as if to say, *He's not coming back yet, but soon.*

Kim-Ly and Huong and I climb into the camper. It smells of bacon fat. My sister looks down at my ankle.

"Him?"

I nod.

"Evil," she says. "Devil man."

"I have to feed her now," I say. But Huong does not take the bottle. She is agitated, keen to take in her new surroundings, her bright eyes focused on her aunt.

"She looks like you," says Kim-Ly.

"She looks like you," I say.

My sister offers me two small blankets and I wrap Huong in them until all I can see are her cheeks and her eyes and a little of her hair.

There is a beating sound outside and through the acrylic window we can see Cynth bashing the chain desperately, swinging a shovel and hitting the heavy metal links over and over again like a coal miner deep below the earth. Her strength is immense. I have no idea where it comes from or how she manages to keep going. There are sparks. But she does not succeed; she throws down the shovel and runs out to find something else.

"How are our parents?" she asks. "Are they well?"

"I don't know," I say. "Kim-Ly, I've been here for years. Right here. Over there."

She shakes her head.

"I got the letters."

She looks up with some absurd and desperate hope in her eyes. "You did!"

"From Manchester, from the nail salon."

She nods. "I thought they were the bad days. But then he brought me out here. This place. Him and his pills."

"Horse pills?" I say.

She frowns.

"Big pills, too big to swallow?"

She points to the three and a half tablets on the Formica fold-down table between the single beds.

"I need two a day now," she says. "He'll bring me two if I'm good. He doesn't forget. I sleep a lot these days, fourteen hours a day or more." She looks at me. "I'm dying from the tablets, I expect. My insides don't work well anymore, Thanh."

I squint my eyes shut and shake my head. Then I open my eyes and look at her chained ankle and I say, "We'll get you to a hospital."

"I spent the first few months screaming like this." She cups her hands around her mouth. "At them, at the cars and vans and trucks on the road. I could see them, but they couldn't see me or hear me. Too far away. I lost my voice from all the screaming. And he lost his temper. I'd only get things—toothpaste, a blanket, a bar of soap—if I stayed quiet. But I can live without those things, I've lived without them for years." She points to the dusty horse tablets. "But those I cannot live without. Not anymore. They control me more than he does."

I think back to the sound of pigs screaming. The desperate hungry screeching noises carried on the damp sea air. That was Kim-Ly? Did I hear my own sister those nights?

I look out the window at Cynth working, bashing the chain over and over again with a rock.

"Were there ever pigs here?" I ask.

Kim-Ly shivers and her face contorts.

"Never?" I say.

"Yes," she says. "There were lots of pigs."

Thank God. It was the pigs screaming. It was just the pigs.

"He sold them?"

She looks at me and screws up her face into a tight knot. She shakes her head.

"He had a wife, you see."

"Jane?" I say.

"Jane," she says.

"What's that got to do with the pigs?"

"Jane died, Thanh. Before I arrived here."

"I know."

Kim-Ly shakes her head. "She died. I have no idea how. Maybe he killed her, maybe she killed herself, I don't know anything."

I nod, rocking Huong in the crook of my arm.

"One night when I was screaming at the cars in the distance, he told me how, years ago, he left her with them."

My mouth falls open.

"You mean?" I say.

She nods.

"But the next day he told me he was only joking. To scare me," she says. "Thanh, I don't know what the real truth is. He might have left her to the pigs."

I feel faint. I take a deep breath to steady myself. I must not pass out now, not now.

"Over the years," says Kim-Ly, shaking her head, tears in her eyes. "There was no other food. He told me it was a lie. Just a joke. He told me the pigs ate scraps, that's all."

I hold my hand out to her and she takes it and she's shaking.

"There's a freezer here somewhere. He froze them. I refused to eat the pork he gave me." She swallows and nods toward the kitchen at the far end of the camper, at the electric oven. "In case it was true. But I got so hungry, Thanh. I would have died. I was too weak, my hair was falling out. I told myself, with the first cut of meat, it had just lived on vegetable scraps. That's all. Nothing else."

"It's true," I say. "That is true, Kim-Ly."

"But I'll never know for sure."

I bite my lip and look down at my child.

"I know for sure," I say, lying, doing something for my sister, offering her some peace, something solid to anchor to. "He told me what happened to Jane, his first wife. The pigs here just ate scraps. Nothing else."

She closes her eyes with relief and squeezes my hand.

"There's nothing that'll work," says Cynth, panting, interrupting this horror, her filthy head peering through the fiberglass camper door. "Jane, can I talk to you?"

I take my child out to Cynth, outside the camper, the thick unbroken chain still in her blackened hands.

"We can't break this, not even close," Cynth says between breaths. "Jane, we have to run for it. Your sister can't come with us right now, she can't leave this spot, but we can. We have to. Let's run to the road, this barn in between us and the cottage, and we'll get help. The police. Or a farmer. We'll come back here and help her right away, I promise."

I look out at the road and Huong looks up at me, I can feel her eyes on mine.

"I can't leave my sister."

"We'll come back for her later today."

"You don't understand, Cynth. She's been here alone for years. Alone. My own baby sister." Tears threaten behind my eyes. "I will never leave her again. Never. We have to stay together. If we go find help and he comes back he'll kill her. He'll hide it all."

Cynth throws her hands in the air.

"We will die," she says, her chin trembling.

"Bolt cutters," I whisper.

"What?"

I look at her and smile and then that smile morphs into a grimace as I feel every inch of the journey in my ankle, in my knees, in my hips, in my back.

"Bolt cutters, in the shed by the cottage. We go back, bring them here, free Kim-Ly. We leave this place together. All of us."

Cynth shakes her head.

"You'll never make it all the way back there," she says. "Neither will I. And he'll be on his way back from town; he'll be getting hungry for his dinner by now, Jane. You know it yourself."

"We have to try. If there's two of us we can fight him. We can fight."

"I'll go get help," she says. "It's a better plan. I'll run to the road by myself and call for help and then I'll come straight back."

I stare toward the road and there are no cars on it. No trucks, no motorbikes, no tractors, no buses, no nothing.

I shake my head.

"I can't go back into that cellar," she says, raw panic in her eyes, her shoulders seeming to fall away from her. "Not down there again. Not that place."

"I'll leave Huong with my sister," I say, nodding to myself, and then I hear my own words and I am astonished and also not surprised at all. I have never been more than twenty feet from Huong. And yet the thought of leaving her in the care of Kim-Ly fills me with hope, not terror. I'll leave the bottle. I'll show her how Huong likes to be rocked, what noises to make.

"We have to get the bolt cutters, Cynth. We have to leave right now."

I dash into the camper.

"There are tools back at the cottage, bolt cutters," I tell her. "Cynth and I will fetch them and come straight back. I need to leave Huong with you. It'll be faster if it's just the two of us."

She nods and grips my daughter in her arms.

"Thank you," she says.

I turn and Cynth has already fled.

No.

"Cynth!" I shout. "Please, Cynthia. Come back!"

I hobble out to the pig enclosures and she is nowhere.

"I need your help!"

The wind whistles. It tastes of salt.

"I can't make it on my own," I say, my voice failing me, the noise catching in my throat. "I need your help."

She appears from behind the wall. "I know," she says. "I know you do. The coast is clear," she says. "We go together. Let's be quick."

I go back to the camper and take Huong from Kim-Ly and kiss her and breathe in her smell. "This woman is your other mother," I whisper in her tiny, perfect ear. "I told you that I was your aunt and your family and your friends. I was wrong. This is your family." I rub my nose against her plump cheek. "My love."

And then I hand her back to my sister and dare not look at her a last time because then I will surely fail.

I kiss Kim-Ly on her forehead and she says, "Go."

30

I'm being pulled back.

I'm being dragged west toward that miserable cottage for the bolt cutters but also east back to my lost sister and my child. And toward the road. Torn in every direction. It's getting dark now, the sun low on the ground, and I can see headlights flash on and off on that faraway road.

We're walking faster. Kim-Ly gave us each half a horse pill, the rectangular ones, and it's helping. We know exactly how far it is to get to those bolt cutters and that's reassuring, and we know how much is at stake here, how many lives, how many lost years, how many possibilities. We've done this once and we can do it again. We know that we all have actual futures almost within reach, and that helps as well. It fuels us.

There is damp in the air. I keep thinking I can hear Huong cry out for me, but it's the flatland winds being cruel, tricking me. Cynth has her bony arm around my waist. We settle into a rhythm, no talking, just her and me, three good feet between us; two shoes and one sandal.

"Is that him?" she asks.

We walk faster, her shoulder bone piercing into my underarm, and there are lights up on the other road, the bigger road, the road I saw seven years ago when I arrived here.

"That's not him," I say.

The cars are driving, not turning, They're not signaling or maneuvering onto his track, Lenn's track. He's still at the shop. He's not back yet.

"Might be that the bridge is up," says Cynth. "Dear God, I hope it is."

I saw the bridge years ago on the local news, me sitting on the floor, his fingers exploring my scalp. Before Huong. Before he burned my passport and my clothes and the photograph of my extended family. The bridge pivots around to let larger boats travel up the river. The cars have to stop. Maybe he's waiting for it?

We cross a stile in seconds and race off toward the dike.

"Let's cross it together," says Cynth. "Like we walk. Together."

George and Lennie.

We plunge straight into the dark metallic waters. Nothing down there, no eels, no rats, no creature ready to take my sandal. It's muddier than before and even though we cross at a different point this time, I still hope to pick up my size eleven sandal from this stinking black silt.

As we clamber up from the escarpment, back onto the flatness that is every direction, the water streams off us and we drip and slosh and make our own mud under our feet. I slip again and again, and it is Cynth who stops me from falling. She is the size of a baby deer and yet she has the power of a draft horse.

"Keep on going," she says. "That's the way."

It's cold, freezing cold, the air cooling more with each minute, the sun sinking into the earth, collapsing into the spires that have never once helped me and the trees that I have never touched.

He's not here. He is still out there, at the shop, in his Land Rover. We'll get the bolt cutters and run back and free Kim-Ly, and we'll all make it to that back road.

I haven't produced milk for weeks, but my breasts hurt like they did before, they yearn for her. I yearn for her. I look back at the barn and I don't fear for my child, she's with Kim-Ly, but I yearn for her. It's a kind of hurt the horse pills don't touch. I'm a hundred, a thousand times farther away from my baby than I have ever been. Than I will ever be again.

We cross into the winter wheat field and Cynth is slowing. I try to keep up the momentum but I'm half carrying her now, half taking her weight.

"Almost there," I say. "You'll be back in your own house soon, Cynth. Triangular windows. You can put your feet up soon. Come on."

She tries but there's not enough life left in her.

She's loose at the knees, stumbling.

She says nothing.

"I can't make it on my own," I say. "We are relying on each other now, Cynth. One last push. Come on."

"I will not make it back," she says.

"You will. We'll get the cutters and you will make it back, we'll make it back together."

"I'll get you as far as the cottage."

The sad, defeated words float and linger in the damp fenland air. They wait there for the winds to come and blow them out to sea. *I'll get you as far as the cottage.*

There is no woodsmoke. No light. I look back over my shoulder and the barn is dark now in the distance. It is small. They're both in there, in that camper, his mother's and his, they're together inside, no food for her, no formula. I'll collect some in the cottage, it'll only take a minute, thirty seconds.

One last field.

Fertile black soil reclaimed long ago from the seas.

Earth plowed into ridges. They're twice as tall and twice as easy to stumble over as on the way out. No frost yet but it's on its way. Sinking down from the gray skies like a cold sheet of silk.

"He's not coming," says Cynth. "You'll get your cutters."

I say nothing. *You'll* not *We'll*. It's still *We'll*. It still is.

We hobble on, the crunch of last season's barley under our feet. My sock, his mother's sock, is wearing through. I'll have one bare foot for the journey back.

"You go in and get a tub of formula and a pack of rich teas. They're by the sink. I'll get the cutters from the shed." I'm panting now, my lungs aching in my chest. "One minute, then straight back out to them."

She says nothing. Her red hair, once so bright and curly, beautiful, is now black in the twilight. Like ribbons of dried blood. She keeps moving though, everything she has is keeping her moving. She's almost there.

The edge of the field.

We cross through the low hawthorn hedge and I touch the wall of the cottage. We separate. She goes inside and I use the wall to help me around to the shed. The house looks dead tonight, no people, no lights, no heat, no fire. No ham or eggs or fries.

I get to the shed and open the door and reach up for the cutters, my stomach straining as I stretch. I hold them and get a surge of energy from taking these terrible things. They imprisoned me here but now they'll free my sister. We'll call it even.

"Let's go," says Cynth, standing at the doorframe of the shed, her pockets bulging on each side of her legs.

There are lights behind her.

She twists to look over her shoulder and I see the headlights.

His headlights.

"No," she says. "Run."

I fall out of the shed, the cutters in my hands, and close the door and we dash around to the edge of the building. But I already know that this will not work. Not him against us. He will find us in minutes and then he will find them. Four lives over one way or another.

"Get inside," I say.

She looks at me like I'm him.

"Inside. Trust me. We can't go back yet."

She shakes her head. Her voice is as small as a child's. "I can't do it, Jane."

"It won't be for long, trust me."

She's looking at me and then at the headlights and then at me again. The lights go off. He's parked up by the locked halfway gate.

"You know what to do?" she asks. "You'll come for me?"

I nod.

We walk into the house and I want to retch. I'm back here in his cottage. Cold. The camera lights blinking as I walk. I unbolt the door to the half-cellar and Cynth looks at me like she's given up now, like she has nothing left. She steps through and glances back and says nothing.

I bolt the door.

Then I strip naked by the locked TV cabinet, mud splattering the floorboards, and dump my wet clothes under the plastic-wrapped sofa and throw the bolt cutters under there too.

How can I do this?

I have to think, I have to make no mistakes, nothing. I have to protect my family, these three. All of them.

I turn on the bath faucets and run back and get a new box of matches from under the sink and light a fire in the Rayburn stove and open the vents so they're full and blow into the firebox and shiver and fill it with the best willow I can find. I wipe the floor with paper and stuff the brown, muddy paper into the Rayburn and then I clean up some more, mopping up earth and seeds and dike water, burning the paper, removing the signs.

I hear the door open as I'm climbing into the ice-cold bathwater.

His footsteps.

I shake from the freezing water.

The rustle of shopping bags in the kitchen.

"Bleedin' hell, it's cold in here, ain't it?"

I hear him open the firebox of the Rayburn and then close it again.

Footsteps.

Lenn at the open bathroom door.

"When's dinner?"

He's there and I'm here, back here, door open, trying not to shiver in this chilled water, trying not to let my teeth shake together in my mouth.

"Half an hour," I say.

"Make sure it is," he says. "Better build up that fire. Where's Janey?"

"Nap," I say.

"Alright," he says. "I'll go up and feed the pigs now before dinner."

31

I sit up in the bath and let the water cascade down me.

He looks.

He stands in the doorframe and watches me like he's done every single day for seven years.

"Dinner in fifteen minutes?" I say, my skin covered in bumps. "Bath's run cold, I'm getting out."

"Fifteen?"

I nod, standing up to take a thin, moth-eaten towel, his mother's, and wrapping it around myself. The water is brown but it's okay. It's me he's looking at. Staring. Does he suspect something? His blue-gray eyes are unreadable, always have been. They're dead in his head.

"I'll feed the pigs after," he says. "Make sure them eggs are sloppy, and no hard crust under neither."

"Yes," I say.

He sits down at the computer in the main room and switches it on.

No wrong moves, not a single one.

I hobble to the bottom stair, my body yearning for Huong. Why is she not with me? My soul feels depleted. Hollow. Then I say, "There's a dead pheasant outside by the hawthorn hedge."

He looks at me. "Dead, dead?"

I nod.

He sniffs and gets up and walks outside. He puts the dead things in the nettle patch by the septic tank; he doesn't like dead things in his garden.

I inch upstairs, my ankle a third bigger than usual. The cuts on the other sole have clotted in the chill of the bathwater. I get to the top of the stairs, to the small back bedroom. There's a ghostly light up here. A stillness. I've already said goodbye to this rotten place and I shouldn't be back here. I pull the pillows into a kind of square in the single bed and ruck the sheets underneath. I get to the storage closet, left side empty, right side his mother's things. I take a few cloths. His mother's cloths. Used by me and used by Huong, but they are and always will be his mother's cloths. I roll them into a baby shape and stuff them under the sheets in the center of the pillows.

By the time he gets back inside, the Rayburn fire is burning hot and the room is warming. But it is still damp. And Cynth is underneath me. Silent. Waiting. What is she thinking down there? We didn't have time to talk about this possibility. Well, we did, but we never managed it. I've already decided we leave here tonight after he's fallen asleep. That's the new plan. Cynth will know what I'm thinking. We'll both arrive at that plan because that's all we can do. As long as he believes Huong is upstairs fast asleep in that back bedroom, then it might work. It just might.

I fry his ham and his eggs and place his fries into his mother's baking tray and slide them into the Rayburn top oven. With every movement, every routine action tried and tested hundreds of times to get it perfect for him, I'm being sucked back here to this place.

My child is over there in the pig barn by the horizon. With my sister. And I am back here in this fenceless prison, this fenland pigpen of his own design.

"Bird's dealt with," says Lenn, walking back in. "Cock pheasant, looked frit to death, it did. Somethin' frit it."

The egg white bubbles and I pop them one by one and feed the fire with more willow.

"Young Janey still sleeping?"

"She's still getting over the sickness. I want her to rest."

"In the back bedroom, is she?"

I nod but my body wants to flee. I am braced against the stainless-steel rail of this Rayburn, his mother's old stove, and I want to take off and flee.

He walks to the banister and looks up.

Time slows.

He goes upstairs.

Don't panic. Keep a clear head.

I have a carving knife on the countertop and the poker resting beside the stove and I know both are useless against him. My ankle throbs. I listen. The floorboards upstairs creak as he moves around. He's in the landing. Now he's in his front bedroom. He's coming downstairs.

"What happened to the rich teas? You ain't finished them, have you? The full package?"

I turn to face him.

My ankle is burning against the firebox and I am sweating at the back of my neck, beads rolling down between my shoulder blades.

"Dropped them in the sink," I say. "They turned to mush. I'm sorry, Lenn."

He looks at me like he's deciding what to do about it, or maybe he's deciding if I'm lying.

"You reckon we should give young Janey a pill from town now or later?" he says.

"The acetaminophen?" I say. "Later. Let her sleep."

"Don't ruin them eggs or we'll have nothin' to eat in the house."

I take the skillet off the hot plate and make up his plate and make up mine. I am so hungry I could eat both, but I have to look normal, like I haven't half escaped; like I don't know my sister is right here, alive, hidden, chained up; like I don't know the horrors he might have inflicted upon his first wife.

"It's alright," he says, pushing his knife into the yolk of an egg like a scientist conducting an experiment. The surface gives. I watch the skin of the yolk indent under the strain and then it bursts and the rich yellow runs over his ham and his fries. "It's alright."

We eat.

Cynth is underneath me right now, exhausted, starving, in the dark. We owe each other everything. George and Lennie.

"You been in the shed today?" he asks.

I cough, the fatty skin of a fry catching in my throat.

"Have some juice, Jane."

I drink the lime juice and my eyes are watering.

"Needed to check—" My voice is strange from the fry skin.

"Wrong hole," says Lenn. "Fry's gone down the wrong hole, is all. Drink your juice."

"Needed to check on the paint," I say. "I want to do the bathroom ceiling again."

He nods and looks at me and moves pink ham into his mouth and chews and keeps on looking at me.

"And?" he says.

"And what, Lenn?"

"Do I need to buy a tin of paint or not? Ain't cheap, you know, that sealin' paint. Bit a rot on the wall won't hurt her. Janey's as strong as her father, she'll have lungs like a boar pig."

"We're fine," I say. "There's some paint left in the tin."

My God, Huong. Are you okay? I know you're safe with Kim-Ly, but what are you feeling right now, what are you thinking? I have not left you. I have not betrayed you. I am still your family and your neighbors and your teachers and your friends. I always will be.

"People are out there searchin' again in the town. Posters are up with her picture."

I stay quiet. I don't want to set him off.

"Ain't good, Jane."

He looks down at the floorboards and I glance out the window in the direction of my daughter and my sister.

"You think you know somethin'," he says. "But sometimes you don't, do you?"

I look at the stove. At the poker.

"You think things are alright, cuz they always have been, but you never really know what's happenin', do you?"

I look down at my empty plate, my pulse beating faster, the yolk stains dry on his mother's plate.

"Especially when somethin's perfect, really working well, never a problem, and then stuff gets changed, do you understand?"

A scratch from the half-cellar below.

I look at him. His face is as expressionless as a wall.

"They stopped sellin' Arctic roll in the shop. Not just in the big shop after the bridge neither, in the Spar shop down in the village and all. Tried three shops in the end. The Spar shop said they can't get it, the big shop after the bridge reckons it'll be comin' in next week, the butcher place in the village inland reckons the factory

went bust. Been havin' that for me puddin' last thirty-odd years on
and off, and then it all just stops, you know?"

I clear his plate and my plate.

"Sure Janey's alright?" he says. "Ain't heard a peep from her."

"She's tired, but I think her fever's passed," I say. "I'll go and
check on her."

"Yeah," he says. "I'll get off and feed the pigs."

He puts the leftovers, ham fat and rind, into the scraps bucket,
and then he goes into the bathroom and closes the door. I pull myself
up the banister and peer into the empty back bedroom, at the fake
child sleeping in the single bed, and then I inch back down to the
Rayburn.

I can't let him go to the pig barn.

I pick up the poker and stoke the fire until the end glows red but
then I set it back down again.

The toilet flushes.

He comes out wiping his hands on his overalls, looking at me.

"Well?" he says.

"What?"

"Janey doin' alright now, or not?"

"Oh, she's fine. She'll be awake soon."

"House is cold today, ain't it? When I got back from the shops
uptown, it were colder inside than out."

I look at the Rayburn. I pick up some willow sticks, my hands
shaking, and feed the fire and open the vents.

"You think I'm stupid?" he says.

I shake my head. "No, no, of course I don't."

"That fire ain't been lit for hours, Jane. Me house had frost in it."

"I'll keep it going, I promise. I'll not let it go out again."

"Nothin' left of yours to burn on it, is there?"

I am so tired of this. Tired in my bones and in my head.

"No," I say. "Nothing."

"That why?"

"Is that why I let the fire go out?"

"That why you didn't do your jobs today?"

"Yes," I say. "I'm sorry. I slept with the baby upstairs because she was sick. I'm sorry, Lenn."

He nods and picks up the scraps bucket. Then he places it back down and swallows and says, "That why you opened the door down to the cellar?"

"What?" I push myself back toward the Rayburn.

"Bolts been opened, they've been moved."

The fire scorches the backs of my legs.

"No," I say. "I wouldn't."

He looks down into the scraps bucket and then back up at me and then up to the ceiling.

"Quiet up there, ain't it?"

I smell something. The Rayburn.

"Saw you both when I come home. Two of you in me headlights, comin' out of the shed."

No. I shake my head but my knees are loose, they're not keeping me upright. My daughter. My sister. My friend.

"No, Lenn," I say, and then I lower my voice. "She's still down there." I point to the floor and frown. There's smoke rising through the paper-thin gaps in the floorboards, gray wisps rising and being pushed by the draft from the door.

He drops the bucket and runs to the half-cellar door.

32

He unbolts the top bolt. Says nothing.

I'm right behind him.

There is gray smoke drifting from under the door.

He unbolts the bottom bolt and the door swings open.

Thick smoke.

He coughs and moves forward and I see something red down by my feet. Cynth's hair. She's curled up in a ball at the top of the ladder, down by his boots, with her scarf wrapped around her mouth.

Lenn moves his arm around to clear the smoke.

I lean back.

I surge forward and push into his solid wall of a back and he stumbles into the slate-gray smoke and Cynth rises and bucks and we push him down there and we scream.

He's gone.

Down the ladder.

Disappeared into the smoke. He's down there and we're up here.

I pull Cynth close and slam the door to the half-cellar shut and reach to lock the upper bolt as Cynth does the same down near the floor. But she's too slow. She's wheezing for air and she's too slow. She coughs something up. The door bulges down below, straining on its hinges. The frame flexes in the wall, the timbers creaking. He bangs his fist. We both lean, pushing into the bottom half of the door with all our weight, my one good foot straining against the wall for leverage. He heaves and we push back. Black smoke now curls up from under the door. He bangs at it again with his fist and Cynth screams as she tenses her arm and heaves the bolt shut.

It's quiet.

He isn't saying a word.

The door bangs again, a new attempt to barge through the big black iron bolts but he cannot do it. Not from that angle. Not without a run-up. Not from the ladder. He is down there and we are up here.

"Burned my fleece," says Cynth. "With your matches." She shows me the box of Swan Vestas.

"Your fleece?"

She nods.

The smoke is still rising up into the main room, through the gaps in the floorboards, under the computer table, snaking around the legs of the two pine chairs and the pine table, billowing from under his armchair, from under the plastic-wrapped sofa.

The floor bulges and shakes as he thrashes around to break through, to break up into this ground-floor room.

I crouch down and drag out the bolt cutters from under the sofa.

Dust and smoke mix together in the air.

"Help me to get upstairs," I say. "Help me up."

Cynth shakes her head. "We have to go," she says. "Your baby, your sister."

"Help me upstairs."

She helps me.

The house is getting hot, getting hotter than I've ever felt it even in the middle of August when the dike runs dry and the grass bleaches white-yellow.

More bangs from under the house. His shoulder smashing into doors and floorboards. His body a battering ram.

I open the linen closet in his bedroom and take out the thin cotton sheet and his small towel. We get down the stairs and the cast-iron Rayburn is glowing red. I open the firebox door and the flames flare out into the room, and I throw in the sheet and the towel and I close the fire door. The stove, his mother's stove, devours them.

His possessions burn.

I take two things with me: the bolt cutters and a tub of formula, the tub he bought for Huong this afternoon from the town past the bridge.

The smoke rises through the floorboards like Cynth's pleas and whispers once did.

We step outside into the cold, clear night.

Heat at my back.

We turn left, as one, to face the wind turbines on the horizon. We walk, as one, past the wall of the cottage, past the Rayburn ash pile, which is also the resting place of all seventeen of my lost possessions. Cynth helps me as we skirt past the hawthorn hedge and the eel remains. The bolt cutters feel good in my hand. The formula bulges from my apron, his mother's apron.

There's woodsmoke in the air.

We turn, my friend and I, heat at our backs, and set off toward the barn, toward my sister and my child.

EPILOGUE

I'm not celebrating the one-year anniversary of his death. I'm celebrating the one-year anniversary of my life. Our lives. All four of them.

I bleach the sink and it's a joy. No cameras watching my every move. No oversight.

The words of Steinbeck mingle with the bleach fumes. An audiobook playing through my phone. My own phone. The contract is in my name. My actual name. I still have the box and all the original packaging. I keep it in a closet upstairs. On one side are my things. My treasures. The copy of *Of Mice and Men* gifted to me by Cynth and her new boyfriend at Christmas. My insurance card, wrapped in yellow tissue paper. The letter granting me leave to remain. Next to my things are Huong's things. I guard each precious item like a Rottweiler. Her birth certificate listing me as her mother and showing to the world her real name. Her given name. A radical gift I passed to her back in the cottage.

I rinse the sink and take a moment to look out the window. No fenland fields here. Just a small town that locals want to escape from but that I will love forever. Young entangled couples and pubs and laughing children and coffee shops and the kind of parks where people chat as their kids find common ground by the swings. Old people wheel their shopping home at their own pace. Life comingling and free to shape itself.

Frank Trussock will remain in prison for over a decade.

The lawyers and police told me I didn't have to appear in court. They said I could give written testimony or appear on a screen from another place. But I insisted. I wanted to be there in that courtroom in front of an official judge and in front of Frank Trussock. Facing him. Eye to eye. I testified the best I could as to what he and Lenn were part of. I answered the lawyer's questions and I held my composure. Kim-Ly did the same. At the end of that courtroom day I slept for fifteen hours straight.

When they raided Frank Trussock's farm they found three held against their will. Another six when they raided places his associates controlled. They found a cannabis farm outside King's Lynn in a boarded-up building that used to be a betting shop. But the workers escaped before the raid. Sometimes I think it's a shame they ran away. Maybe I could have helped them. Guided them through all the paperwork and interviews. Helped to find them a safe home.

There's a bang in the next room so I hobble through. One operation done but the three main procedures are still ahead of me. I've been given a prescription for pain management. Proper pills for humans.

Huong looks at me with her beautiful brown eyes and she laughs. Trailing behind her is a train of sorts, a line of her toys all taped together like a snake. The snake knocked the TV remote off the coffee table.

"Uh-oh, Mommy."

The smile on my face is so broad and deep it stretches my skin. She smiles back.

Huong can say "Mommy" in Vietnamese and in English. Her English accent is already better than mine. She is a wonder.

She walks toward me still dragging plastic swords and teddy bears and drinking bottles all taped together.

She stands at my feet, her soft, perfect arms raised in the air.

I brace myself and pick her up.

The weight of her is a miracle. A blessing. A godsend. She is healthy despite all the horse pills, and somewhere deep inside myself I feel that she is well past the danger point. The doctors have confirmed this. She is no longer a vulnerable baby. She's a strong girl now. Resilient. Able to cope with whatever lies ahead. She is a powerful fighter born in the worst place imaginable and yet she thrives.

I pucker my lips and she meets them with her own. Like the gentlest of kisses placed on a mirror.

She has a name and an ID number. She is in the system and she's been vaccinated and she has a dedicated person at social services who checks on her. Regularly. I like that. Other mothers in my situation, people I deal with through my job, they resent the State involvement. But to me it is another level of protection for my Huong. She has me. She has the State. And in between she has my sister and her godmother, Cynth, and she has her grandma back in Biên Hòa who has taught herself how to Skype so she can talk to and cry with joy at the vision of her beloved granddaughter.

But Huong will never meet her grandfather.

He died the year before our escape. Heart failure. Part of me wonders whether the loss of his daughters for all those years ruined his heart. The other part of me knows that it did.

I give Huong a chunk of cucumber. With her beautiful new teeth she can devour a length of cucumber like a beaver might devour a log.

I still get chills.

They might be panic attacks or PTSD. They might just be my bones remembering. But when I walk through this small town I sometimes get chills. We're about an hour from Lenn's farm but the accents are almost the same. If I hear a man say "Don't be stupid" or "What are you talking about?" I stop dead. My blood coagulates in my veins and I have to force myself to breathe deeply and to carry on living. One time I almost passed out with fear when I found cod in parsley sauce in the freezer of the corner shop. I held it cold and stiff in my hands and it sent me straight back there. To that little cottage. That upstairs back bedroom. The locked halfway gate and the eel and the ash pile. The lumpy, damp floor of the lean-to bathroom.

We were saved by a farmer.

A kind bearded man in a pickup truck driving back from some meeting about sugar beet processing. Cynth was the one who flagged him down. Her arms spread wide, her body upright in the middle of the unlit road. I had Huong close to my chest. She was so cold that night. So tiny. Kim-Ly still dragged a length of her broken ankle chain behind her. I can remember the sound of it scraping along the asphalt. Cynth pleaded with the farmer in the truck. He looked horrified. The whites of his eyes that night. He helped us all into his pickup and he turned the heat up high. That farmer gave us his Mars bar and his bottle of Coca-Cola. He drove us to the nearest police station. He even waited outside to check that we were okay.

We were not okay. But in time we would be.

What saves me is people. Strangers. Old women. Shopkeepers. Young lovers and milkmen doing their rounds and window cleaners with ladders fixed on top of their vans. Individuals oblivious to one another and yet, in a way, together, they act like insurance. An invisible web. Nothing too bad will happen on the street of a small town like this because people are everywhere. If something heinous occurs, then it's likely to be short-lived. Terrible acts are more difficult to conceal in a place like this. Someone will eventually step in or call the police. Horrors can still take place, but people look after people even though they might never think of it that way.

Huong takes the TV remote and changes the channel. We all get a say in what we watch. Kim-Ly is obsessed with competitive cooking programs and I don't tell her I'm hooked, too, but I am. The simple act of choosing a channel. Making that decision. All of us enjoying the selection. That simple act of togetherness.

I prefer documentaries and news programs. But never the snooker or *Match of the Day*. I avoid them both. Something visceral about the theme tunes. Even with my sister and my daughter in the room, the front door locked, not a living enemy in the free world, those theme tunes can send me straight back to sitting at his feet, his Rayburn fire door open, his hands in my hair.

The door opens.

"Snake!" says Huong.

Kim-Ly looks at me and smiles and then puts down her handbag and her keys and falls to the floor with her niece, hissing and laughing and tugging at the line of taped possessions.

"Half an hour," I say. "How was work?"

"Not bad," she says. "There might be an assistant manager job opening up next year."

"Can you still do that with all your studies?"

"Of course I can," she says.

There is still a scar on her ankle. A groove. There is no twisted knot of bone and gristle, but she bears the marks of her trauma just like I do.

Huong turns the volume up on the TV and Kim-Ly turns it back down again. I dress Huong in her party dress with her black patent leather shoes and her golden sheriff badge. Kim-Ly showers and puts on a jumper I bought her for Christmas, and a skirt she found in the charity shop on Main Street. Her short, beautiful hair is wet at the tips. Pop music plays low in the background and the apartment is full of easy happiness.

Huong takes a card from the coffee table. It's a photograph of Cynth riding her horse and it has a big purple heart on the other side.

We take out the food and the drinks and Kim-Ly drops a glass. We clean it up.

I check on the *phở* broth.

The doorbell rings.

Huong runs squealing and Kim-Ly unlocks the door.

Red hair. Freckles. Jodhpurs. A squeal as Cynth picks Huong up off the floor and holds her up to look at her.

The familiar dial tone of a Skype call bleeps from my phone and Huong squeals again.

My world in this apartment.

My family.

AFTERWORD

If you suspect someone is in need of support as a result of human trafficking, exploitation, or their migration status, then the following organizations may be able to assist:

International Rescue Committee
www.rescue.org

The Young Center for Immigrant Children's Rights
www.theyoungcenter.org

World Relief
www.worldrelief.org

ACKNOWLEDGMENTS

Heartfelt thanks:

To my mother.

To my friends and family.

To my agent, Kate Burke, and everyone at Blake Friedmann.

To my screen agent, James Carroll, and everyone at Northbank.

To my US editor, Emily Bestler, and the whole Emily Bestler/Atria/Simon & Schuster team.

To my UK editor, Jo Dickinson, and the whole Hodder team.

To Hayley Webster, Bethany Rutter, and Liz Barnsley for reading early drafts.

To all the librarians, booksellers, international publishers, bloggers, reviewers, event organizers, and translators.

To Thanhmai Bui-Van. For your wise, generous words.

To Maxine Mei-Fung Chung. For your kind, encouraging words.

To my wife and son. I love you.

Turn the page for an exclusive excerpt
from Will Dean's latest novel,
First Born

I am half a person.

The darkest half. The half that isn't quite 50 percent.

It's time to check my fire alarm, so I stand up on my mattress and press the test button. It bleeps. I test it again because I read on Quora one time—a comment embedded deep inside a thread—that it's possible to get a false positive.

Sometimes I feel like I am a false positive.

Not sometimes. For at least eighteen of the past twenty-two years. Since I was four years old. That's when I realized two important things in life. First: there are no such things as identical twins. Second: the universe conspires to trip you up.

I test the alarm one more time and it bleeps.

I lie back down on the bed and the four baby-safe pillows compress under the weight of my head. Pillows made with air holes. Breathable pillow slips. It's rare that a full-grown adult woman suffocates from lying facedown in her sleep, but it is not impossible. There was a reported case in South Korea last year.

On my bedside table rests a knife with a three-inch blade. It's legal because it does not lock and the blade is short, but I made sure to order the toughest knife available. It's a balance of risks. Being incarcerated, even short-term, even just being questioned by the police, versus the risk of being violently attacked in my own home.

My entire existence is made up of balancing risks. KT, my twin, has never felt the need.

I want to move to the kitchen to make a cup of tea, but I will not leave while my phone is charging. Reddit taught me better. A retired firefighter shared his top three tips for avoiding house fires. This wasn't his opinion; it was his conclusion after years of experience. First: avoid electric bed blankets. Second: avoid cheap Christmas lights. Third: never leave your phone charging on a flammable surface. I don't watch my phone the whole time it's charging, I'm not insane, but I do lie or sit next to it, within arm's reach of my fire extinguisher and emergency fire blanket. There's another pair of extinguishers in the far corner of the room. Another pair in every other room of my small Camden Town apartment. I believe in forward planning.

Camden may not be known as the safest area of London, but again, there is a balance to be found. Most people look at crime statistics and property prices and then they make their decision. I need to avoid crime and I need to avoid bankruptcy, both serious risks living here. I'm also mindful of other pertinent factors. My real estate agent was more than a little surprised when I asked for the exact elevation above the River Thames. Like he hadn't heard about rising sea levels. Like he hadn't watched the documentary by a Dutch scientist on YouTube about how the Thames Flood Barrier is already outdated and how if we suffer a once-in-a-century storm surge much of London will end up underwater.

When I calculate my budget, I always try to keep some money back for Mum in case she ever needs it again. Five years ago Dad's business almost went under. Mum has no job, no qualifications, no income. He doesn't want her to work. I don't feel comfortable with that setup, that lack of autonomy, so I try to save a few pounds each month in case she ever needs it.

Next to my phone is a photo of them both. My parents: Paul and Elizabeth Raven. Good people. Caring and straightforward and down-to-earth. Honest, mostly. Mum is, at least. Next to that is a photo of me, Molly Raven, and my monozygotic twin, Katie, or, as I call her, KT. I don't use the term *identical twin* because it's a blatant lie. A travesty. Our base DNA is identical, sure, but that's about all that is.

We were once one person.

We are not anymore.